"What will you do if you don't hire a doctor to stand in for Tom?"

Stacy didn't even hesitate. "Keep your fingers crossed that doesn't happen, because then we'll have to shut down until we find someone."

Mark's conscience pricked, but why he felt responsible for what wasn't his problem was anyone's guess. Regardless, he wasn't about to let the fact that Saddlers Prairie needed a doctor stop him from flying to L.A. and the great job awaiting him. Pushing the guilt aside, he said, "If I think of someone, I'll let you know."

They stood together on the porch, under the yellow overhead light.

"Here we are again," he said. "Saying good-night."

Unable to keep his hands off her, he tucked her hair behind her ears, just as he had last night. His fingers traced the delicate shells of her ears.

Her lips parted a fraction, but her gaze fixed on his chest, as if she were scared to look at him.

"Hey, Stace." Mark feathered her cheek with his thumb, then gently raised her chin so that she was forced to meet his gaze.

"I'm going to kiss you now.

Dear Reader,

Welcome to Saddlers Prairie, a fictitious town in Montana prairie country, and home of my new miniseries. Though many of my family members are physicians, this second book in the miniseries is my first story ever featuring a doctor.

After a bad breakup, Stacy Andrews left her home and moved to Saddlers Prairie. She now works at the only medical clinic for miles around. Her boss is nearly seventy-five and ready to retire, but finding a doctor to take over the small-town clinic isn't so easy.

Enter Dr. Mark Engle. Mark is about to leave Montana for good, begin a lucrative medical career in another state and never look back. However, things happen, and when he… But telling you now won't be nearly as much fun as reading the details for yourself.

I loved sharing Stacy and Mark's story, and hope you'll enjoy it, too.

I always appreciate hearing from readers. Email me at ann@annroth.net, or write me c/o P.O. Box 25003, Seattle, WA 98165-1903. I invite you visit my website at www.annroth.net, where you can enter the monthly drawing to win a free book! You'll also find my latest writing news, tips for aspiring writers and a delicious new recipe every month.

Happy reading!

Ann Roth

Montana Doctor

ANN ROTH

TORONTO NEW YORK LONDON
AMSTERDAM PARIS SYDNEY HAMBURG
STOCKHOLM ATHENS TOKYO MILAN MADRID
PRAGUE WARSAW BUDAPEST AUCKLAND

To the wonderful physicians in my family—my beloved maternal grandfather, gone but never forgotten, my father, my uncle, my two brothers and my daughter. I love and admire you all.

Recycling programs
for this product may
not exist in your area.

ISBN-13: 978-0-373-75412-0

MONTANA DOCTOR

Copyright © 2012 by Ann Schuessler

www.Harlequin.com

Printed in U.S.A.

ABOUT THE AUTHOR

Ann Roth lives in the greater Seattle area with her husband. After earning an MBA she worked as a banker and corporate trainer. She gave up the corporate life to write, and if they awarded PhDs in writing happily-ever-after stories, she'd surely have one.

Ann loves to hear from readers. You can write her at P.O. Box 25003, Seattle, WA 98165-1903 or email her at ann@annroth.net.

Books by Ann Roth
HARLEQUIN AMERICAN ROMANCE

* Saddlers Prairie

OPAL FARRADAY'S BLUE RIBBON APPLE PIE

(with a huge nod to the Barefoot Contessa)

One unbaked deep-dish pie crust

Filling:

*4 lbs apples (Opal suggests using half Granny Smith, half
Pink Lady)*

1 tsp orange zest

1 tsp lemon zest

1 tbsp orange juice

½ cup sugar (heaping, if the apples are sour)

¼ cup unbleached flour

1 tsp salt

¾ tsp cinnamon

½ tsp nutmeg

⅛ tsp allspice

Preheat oven to 400°F. Line a deep-dish pie pan with unbaked
pie crust.

Peel apples and slice. Place in a large bowl; sprinkle with zests and
orange juice and mix to combine. In a separate bowl combine
sugar, flour, salt, cinnamon, nutmeg and allspice. Add to apples,
mixing to combine.

Pour into unbaked pie shell. Top with second crust. (Opal prefers
a lattice crust.)

Bake 60 to 75 minutes. Serve warm or cold, with heavy cream
or ice cream.

Chapter One

Eager to leave Montana for good, Mark Engle sped down the empty highway, toward the Billings airport. The flight to L.A. left at seven, and he was still a good four-hour drive away.

He should've left Steer Bluff earlier, but his mom had treated him to lunch. Mark hated that she spent her hard-earned money on his send-off meal. At least she had a means of getting around now—the old but reliable car that had taken him through med school, a three-year internship/residency at Sheridan County Hospital and a two-year stint there as a family-practice doctor.

Overhead, the dark clouds suddenly opened up. Furious rain bounced off the road and pummeled Mark's rented sedan. Given that this was May in Montana, it was no big surprise. The pavement was slick now, and he slowed down and turned the wipers to high speed.

On either side of him, the celery-green prairie grass and spring flowers bowed under the onslaught. No doubt, the steep drainage ditches lining the road would soon fill with churning water.

A Josh Ritter song started on the iPod and Mark sang along, vaguely noting the white sedan advancing toward him. He thought about his new life in L.A. One week from today, he would start his dream job at Archer Clinic, a private facility for the wealthy that paid a hefty salary and a few years down the road offered the chance to buy a stake in the business. Provided the other partners approved.

He was in hock up to his ears, but at last he could pay down his massive student loans and start a savings account so that when the time came he'd have the funds to buy into the clinic. Meantime, he'd work extra hard to convince the existing partners of his value. He also intended to purchase his first-ever brand-new car, and date lots of gorgeous females—women who understood the importance of putting your career firs—

Without warning, the white sedan veered into his lane. Mark gripped the wheel and swerved to the side of the road. Mere inches from the ditch, his car screeched and skidded to a stop.

The other car didn't fare so well. With a sickening *bam!* it slammed headfirst down the incline.

Mark jumped from his car. Heedless of the rain, he jogged toward the sedan. The front end was rammed against the far side of the ditch, and the back end hovered a few inches off the ground. The air bag had deployed, pinning an elderly woman in place. She was unconscious.

Swearing, he slipped and slid his way down to her. Cold, murky water, already ankle-high, seeped rapidly into his sneakers and soaked the bottoms of his jeans.

Mark checked her pulse. To his relief he found one, though it was weak. He lifted one of her eyelids. Peered at her. "Can you hear me?"

The woman groaned.

"Hang on." He pulled his cell phone from his hip pocket and called 911. "This is Dr. Mark Engle. I'm on the highway, south of—" He broke off to squint at an exit sign a few yards away. "Saddlers Prairie. An elderly female just crashed into a drainage ditch. Unconscious, but coming to now. Pulse thready. Send an ambulance, stat."

"Our closest hospital, Flagg Memorial, is twenty-five

miles west of where you are," the dispatcher said. "It'll be a few minutes."

"What about EMTs from the fire department?"

"They're out on another call."

"Great, just great," Mark muttered, and hung up.

The woman's eyes were open now. A faded blue, and unfocused. "What is this thing in my face?" she asked, feebly pushing at the air bag.

"Don't move—you might have a broken neck. You crashed into the ditch and your air bag deployed."

"Take it off me."

"Do. Not. Move," Mark repeated. "The medics will deflate it when they arrive." He hunkered down to eye level. "What's your name?"

"Florence Jones."

"Age?"

"Seventy-three."

"Is there someone I can call?"

"Dr. Tom." She recited the number.

"Is he a family member?" Mark asked.

"With a name like that? Of course not. He's my doctor."

"Is there any family?"

"I don't… I think so. Where am I, and who are you?"

"My name is Dr. Mark Engle. You ran off the highway, near the Saddlers Prairie exit."

"At least I'm close to home." Florence Jones closed her eyes.

"Stay with me," Mark said.

"Oh, I'm here, all right. I'm going to take a nap now."

Not wanting her to do that, Mark said, "Please keep your eyes open while I contact Dr. Tom."

He dialed the number the woman had provided, which connected, thank God.

"Saddlers Prairie Medical Clinic. This is Stacy," a crisp, female voice said.

Mark pictured a youngish woman with a take-charge expression and dark hair pulled severely back from her face. "Dr. Mark Engle here—I need to speak with Dr. Tom..." Not knowing the man's last name, he let his voice trail off.

"Dr. Sackett is with a patient. Can he call you back?"

Sackett. Mark mentally stowed the name in his memory. "Would you let him know that one of his patients, a Miss—"

"Mrs.," the elderly woman corrected.

"Mrs. Florence Jones has been in a car accident. She just came to, and we're waiting for the ambulance."

"Why didn't you say so?" The woman's tone stopped just short of a scold. "Hold on."

Moments later, Tom Sackett picked up. "I've treated Florence for decades," he told Mark. "She may have had a stroke. Tell her I'll get hold of her son and daughter, and they'll meet her at the hospital."

Before long, sirens filled the air. Flashing bright lights, the ambulance sped down the highway, followed by a sheriff's car.

By the time the EMTs loaded Florence Jones into the ambulance and Sheriff Gabe Bennett finished questioning Mark, the tow truck had arrived and the rain had stopped.

Mark was soaked and cold clear through. He'd also missed any chance of catching his flight to L.A. He trudged to his car to pull fresh clothing from his suitcase and changed quickly with the trunk up. He was zipping the fly of his dry jeans and about to toe into a pair of loafers, when his cell phone rang.

"This is Tom Sackett," the doctor said. "Thanks for taking care of Florence. Heard you missed your plane."

Mark wasn't surprised that the doctor knew about his flight. In small towns, news spread quickly. "There's another flight tomorrow afternoon. I'll fly out then," he said.

An afternoon flight would give him plenty of time to make the trip to Billings in the morning.

"You missed that plane because you were helping my patient. The least I can do is treat you to dinner. Why don't you stop by my clinic. I'll show you around and we'll leave from there."

Mark had zero interest in touring the man's clinic, but as he was stuck in Montana for one more night, he saw no reason why he shouldn't take Tom up on his offer. The country doctor might know of a decent place to bunk for the night.

"Why not?" he said. "Tell me how to find you, and I'll be right over."

"STACY, THE GRAY SEDAN just pulled into the parking lot!"

Dr. Engle had arrived.

"Thanks, Mrs. Card." Stacy Andrews dashed from the kitchen in the back to the reception desk mere seconds before Dr. Engle exited his car.

They'd been expecting him since Dr. Tom's announcement that he'd invited the man to tour the clinic and then have dinner. He was just passing through, but you never knew....

An opportunity like this rarely came along, and Stacy meant to take full advantage of it.

She'd spent the past thirty minutes tidying up. Her desk, which she always kept neat and clean, was even more orderly than usual. In cheery welcome, she'd transferred the bouquet of flowers she'd brought in this morning from the window-sill to her desk.

Though it was after five and Mrs. Card was waiting for her mother, Dr. Tom's last patient of the day, Stacy had started a fresh pot of coffee—the gourmet blend she saved for special occasions. She'd left the kitchen door open, and the mouth-watering aroma filled the waiting room.

She'd also returned the magazines that had migrated to

chairs and side tables to the wall rack, and selected a sooth-
ing, classical-guitar CD for background music. Even Mrs.
Card had gotten into the act, combing her gray-streaked hair
and applying lipstick.

Through the large glass window fronting the reception
area, Stacy watched the doctor start up the walk. He looked
about her age, somewhere in his early thirties. Tall and well
built, with a long, graceful stride. His jeans fit him well,
and his pressed oxford shirt showcased broad shoulders. She
noted his short, dark hair and strong nose, and a squarish
jaw and generous mouth. All of which added up to a handsome man.

Not that Stacy cared. He could've stood five feet tall with
the face of a donkey. The important thing was to convince
the doctor that this clinic was worth his consideration.

As the front door opened, she pasted a welcoming smile on
her face and started her spiel. "Welcome to Saddlers Prairie
Clinic, Dr. Engle. I'm Stacy Andrews, Dr. Tom's receptionist and office manager. He's finishing up with a patient, but
should be out soon."

"Please, call me Mark. You're the woman who answered
the phone earlier."

Intelligent eyes the color of dark chocolate studied her,
and she had the feeling that this man missed nothing. Which
was unnerving, if only because of her ulterior motives. His
looks set her on edge, as well.

Forget merely handsome. Dr. Mark Engle was drop-dead
gorgeous.

For the first time since her ex-fiancé, Vince, had broken
her heart, Stacy felt the stirrings of attraction.

"You look different than you sound," he said.

"Is that good or bad?" she asked, checking her hair, which
was straight and fine textured and always getting in her eyes.

"Neither."

His mouth twitched, as if he knew he'd flustered her. Women probably swooned around him all the time.

Not Stacy. A man's looks had nothing to do with his character—hadn't she learned that lesson in spades? Compressing her lips, she gestured at the empty waiting-room chairs. "Please, make yourself comfortable."

Mrs. Card patted the nubby seat of the chair next to hers. "I'm Debra Card, and I'm waiting for my mother." She lowered her voice. "Hashimoto's disease. Do you know anything about it?"

The doctor nodded. "I've treated a number of patients with the condition. It's a fairly common thyroid problem, and with regular blood tests, easily treatable."

"That's exactly what Dr. Tom says." Mrs. Card beamed. "You're as smart as you are handsome. I can tell you're a wonderful doctor."

"I try."

Mark blushed, charming Stacy. Boy, was she easy. Mentally rolling her eyes, she cleared her throat. "May I get you a cup of coffee, Mark?"

"Black, please."

When she returned with a fragrant, steaming mug, Mrs. Card was talking his ear off.

"—expected you to be a soggy mess from standing in the pouring rain all that time," she said. "Yet here you are, as dry and smartly dressed as if you'd been inside all afternoon. How lucky that you had a change of clothes in your car."

A hint of a smile played at Mark's mouth. "Did you hear about that from the sheriff or one of the medics?"

When Mrs. Card raised her eyebrows, Mark full-out smiled. "I grew up in a town just like this one, and I know that news travels faster than fire in dry brush."

Unabashed, the woman chuckled. "You're absolutely right. Sheriff Bennett told his wife, Louisa. Then she phoned—"

Dr. Tom's door opened with a loud click, silencing Mrs. Card. The clump of a cane announced the patient's slow return to the waiting room. Dr. Tom followed behind her.

"We're all finished," he told Mrs. Card. "Your mother should get her blood checked again in six months. Put that in the appointment book, Stacy." He turned to Mark. "Dr. Engle? I'm Tom Sackett, aka Dr. Tom. This is Mrs. Givens. Welcome to the Saddlers Prairie Clinic."

Mark stood and shook the older woman's hand, then Dr. Tom's.

Clearly struck by the man's good looks, Mrs. Givens simpered. Then she squinted at him through her trifocals. "You'll do quite well."

"Excuse me?" Mark asked.

"Aren't you here to interview for Dr. Tom's job?"

Mark frowned. "I have no idea what you're talking about."

"I'm looking for someone to take over my practice," Dr. Tom explained. "So I can retire."

Stacy hoped he found his replacement soon. Nearly seventy-five and exhausted from years of long hours and minimal time off, the good doctor deserved to relax and enjoy the rest of his "golden years."

Was Mark at all interested? Behind her back, she crossed her fingers and, along with Mrs. Givens, Mrs. Card and Dr. Tom, openly regarded him.

Their hopeful expressions didn't seem to faze him. "Good luck finding someone," he said.

His upper lip actually curled, letting Stacy know exactly what he thought about the Saddlers Prairie practice—that the little clinic was beneath him.

And he wasn't alone. Dr. Tom had been searching for a replacement since before he'd hired Stacy nine months ago. So far, there were no candidates in sight. Practicing small-town medicine didn't seem to interest most doctors.

"I just accepted a job at Archer Clinic in L.A.," Mark said. "I'll be the first family-practice physician Archer has ever had, and they've promised me the opportunity to become a partner." He all but salivated. "I was on my way to the Billings Airport to fly out when Mrs. Jones had her accident."

Having lived in L.A. before relocating to Saddlers Prairie, Stacy knew about the Archer Clinic, a state-of-the-art medical facility on Rodeo Drive that catered to the rich and famous. Looks-wise, Mark would certainly fit in with the clientele, and a partnership would probably make him almost as wealthy as his patients.

Saddlers Prairie Clinic couldn't hope to compete with that. Her heart sank.

But it wasn't just that Saddlers Prairie was a small town. She'd bet a week's salary that Mark Engle was one of those— a smart, handsome male who valued money and prestige above most everything else. Just like Vince. She'd wasted seven years of her life hoping he'd put her first. Never again.

Suddenly she couldn't wait to leave the office and get away from Dr. Mark Engle. There was plenty to do before the day ended. Stop at Spenser's and pick up the yarn for Megan Dawson's baby blanket, putter in the garden and play with Smooth Talker. She'd learned the hard way that when she neglected her pet, he made life unpleasant as only a parrot could, scolding and swearing like a sailor. She also wanted to finish this month's selection before the book-club meeting on Saturday.

While Dr. Tom chatted with Mark, Stacy waved goodbye to Mrs. Givens and her daughter. Using the online appointment book, she added a note six months from now to send the older woman a reminder to get her blood checked.

Then she took her novel and shoulder bag from the desk

Chapter Two

"And that's the twenty-five-cent tour of my clinic," Tom said.

By Mark's calculation, the man had to be at least as old as Florence Jones. Overweight, with tired eyes and a florid complexion. He definitely needed to retire.

"There's a nice two-bedroom apartment upstairs, where I live rent-free," the white-haired doctor continued. "We don't have much in the way of motels here, but even if we did, I'd like you to stay in my guest room tonight."

Needing a place to sleep, Mark readily agreed. "I'll take you up on that."

A smile lit up the older doctor's round face. "Excellent. Let's head out for dinner. On the way there, I'll show you around town."

Mark had no interest in seeing Saddlers Prairie, which probably looked like all the other small ranching towns in eastern Montana. But the tour would help pass the time.

"I'll drive," he offered as Tom locked the clinic door. "Just tell me where we're going, and how to get there."

"Barb's is the best restaurant in town. The *only* restaurant that isn't fast food."

As they headed down the highway, Tom pointed out various ranches. "That one belongs to the Dawson family, one of the few ranches in the area that turns a healthy profit regularly."

"How's the economy around here?" Mark asked.

"Like most every place else—not good."

"The businesses on Rodeo Drive seem to be doing all right."

Tom gave a sage nod. "The rich never suffer like the poor."

Didn't Mark know it. Growing up, he'd been laughed at, teased and taunted by kids whose families were better off.

"See those lights ahead?" Tom pointed out the window. "That's your turn."

Mark pulled into a dirt-packed, half-filled lot that served as the parking area for a group of buildings that included a gas station and a handful of weathered shops. The neon sign for Barb's Café was easy to spot.

He parked in front of Spenser's General Store, a squat building that looked a lot like the general store in Steer Bluff.

Moments later, he and Tom entered the restaurant, a noisy place with an aroma that had his mouth watering. If that wasn't surprise enough, over half the tables were filled. And on a Monday night.

The instant he stepped inside, a hush fell over the room, everyone checking him out. Given that he was a stranger in town, they would. Knowing that didn't make Mark any less uncomfortable. For a moment he was back in Steer Bluff, a scrawny kid in some better-off kid's charity hand-me-downs, walking into the general store with an empty belly and a bagful of discarded returnable bottles he'd collected from the side of the road and the prairie meadows.

Two waitresses, one in her twenties, one middle-aged, approached with a smile. "Hello, Dr. Tom. You must be Dr. Mark. I'm Donna."

"And I'm Autumn," said the younger woman, who was pretty in a scrappy kind of way. "My shift just ended, but I heard what you did for Florence Jones today, and just… That was awesome."

"It really was," Donna said.

Every diner in the place nodded.

Mark dipped his head. "It was nothing."

"Maybe where you're from," Autumn said. "Around here, saving someone's life means something."

She left, and Donna returned her attention to Tom. "Your regular booth is waiting."

Noise filled the room again as the diners resumed their conversations. On the way to the booth, Tom stopped to greet various people and introduce Mark. Everyone had heard of him, and like Autumn and Donna, they all thanked him for helping Florence Jones.

"He's just passing through," Tom explained over and over. "On his way to a job at a fancy clinic in L.A."

After what seemed a good fifteen minutes, they finally reached the booth. Donna handed them menus. "Order whatever you like, but if I were you, I'd go with today's special—Emilio's shepherd's pie," she said. "It's out of this world."

"Trust what this woman says." Tom winked. "She knows what she's talking about. By the way, Emilio is married to Barb. She'd never let him get away with cooking mediocre food."

"All right, then," Mark agreed. "Bring me a shepherd's pie."

"Make that two," Tom said.

Donna inclined her head. "I'll be right back with your salads."

"Where are you from, Mark?" the older man asked as the waitress hurried off.

"A town called Steer Bluff, about a hundred and fifty miles east of here."

"I know the place," Tom said. "That's near Sheridan County Hospital. Did you do your residency there?"

"That's right, and when I finished that, I stayed another two years as a family-practice physician."

"Did you enjoy the work?"

Mark had. He liked working with people, figuring out what was wrong and, when possible, correcting the problem. He nodded.

Dr. Tom looked at him curiously. "You're from Montana. If you don't mind my asking, why are you moving away?"

Because he wanted to leave his impoverished roots behind, start fresh in a new place and make a name for himself. He also wanted to earn piles of money, which was guaranteed once he owned a stake in the clinic.

None of which Tom needed to know. "Except for college and med school, I've always lived in Steer Bluff, and it's time for a change," he explained. "L.A.'s year-round warm temperatures, the fresh fruit and produce, the beautiful women… I can't wait."

Tom's forehead creased as if he were perplexed, and Mark felt compelled to add, "I've had enough of small towns to last ten lifetimes."

"Mind telling me what you have against them?"

"Not at all." Mark counted the reasons on his fingers. "Rampant poverty, a lack of things to do outside work and, worst of all, everybody knowing everyone else's business."

"All true. But there's a positive side, too. Around here, people band together and look out for each other. They tend to have big hearts."

Donna delivered the salads, and Mark and Tom dug in.

Neither spoke while eating, and Mark thought about his old man, who'd had a big heart, especially when he drank. Which had been almost always. But drunk or sober, he'd give every penny of his paycheck to anyone who asked for money, at great cost to his own family.

While he'd breezily doled out cash, Mark's mother had

worked two full-time jobs in a valiant effort to stay ahead of the bill collectors. Unfortunately her jobs never paid well, and sometimes her two paychecks didn't stretch far enough. She'd never had a plan of any kind to keep the family afloat and steer them toward a more prosperous future, and they'd all suffered for it.

For a few years, Mark's grandma had watched over him and his little brother while their mom worked, but Grandma had died when Mark and Kevin were in grade school. From then on, they'd raised themselves.

After her death, Mark often went to bed with an empty belly so that Kevin didn't, and he left for school the next morning in the same condition. He hadn't done much of a job raising his little brother. Kevin had dropped out of high school to become a rodeo rider. Since suffering a serious leg injury, he'd worked on various cattle ranches—when he wasn't drowning in a bottle of gin. The same stuff that'd killed dear old Dad.

Meanwhile, their mom was working two jobs and still doing battle with the bill collectors.

A few moments later, Tom laid down his fork and looked up from his empty salad plate. "I'm curious how you landed the job at Archer Clinic."

Happy to get his mind off his family, Mark shared the story. "Sheer luck. I diagnosed a case of severe anemia in a woman who'd been suffering for months at the hands of a faith healer. Her cousin, a publicist in Hollywood, knew Archer Clinic was looking for a family-practice doc. She recommended me. Back in high school, I developed a life plan that saw me through college and med school. Part of the plan was to push my career in new directions, so I flew to L.A., interviewed and landed the job."

"You sound like a shrewd young man. You must've impressed the hell out of them."

"Let's hope that continues. In order to become a partner, the existing partners have to approve me."

"I'm sure they will. What'd you think of Stacy?"

Wondering at the quick change of subject, Mark thought about Tom's office manager. With chin-length blond hair, a small waist, curvy hips and slender, shapely legs, she wasn't at all the tight-ass librarian type he'd imagined.

He'd always been a sucker for a pretty woman, and had been drawn to her big eyes and warm smile. She'd also seemed to like him—at first. All too soon, she'd turned frosty, but Mark had no idea why. "She seems efficient," he hedged.

"Have you no eyes, man? She's stunning, and also smart." Tom gave his head an admiring shake. "If I were forty-five years younger… But I'm not. She's worked for me since last September, when she moved here from L.A."

"She's from L.A.?" Mark wondered why she hadn't mentioned that. But then, she hadn't had much opportunity. Puzzled and curious as to why she'd traded life in the glamorous city for Podunk, U.S.A., he frowned. "Why in the world did she move to Saddlers Prairie?"

"Jenny Wyler, now Dawson—she married Adam Dawson, whose ranch we passed on the way here—Jenny knew Stacy in college. Last summer, she invited her for a visit. That was after Stacy's fiancé threw her over for a younger woman, and she needed to get away.

"Younger." Tom scoffed. "Stacy wasn't even thirty at the time. She and her then-fella, some hotshot corporate lawyer, were together seven years, and engaged for six of them. He kept postponing the wedding. Told her he wanted to make partner first."

"Makes sense to me," Mark said. "I grew up dirt-poor. Poverty is no fun."

"Poverty isn't always about money, son. Take me. I do all

right. Sure, compared to many doctors my earnings are pea-
nuts. Hell, some of my patients pay me in beef, homemade
bread or a knitted sweater. But they depend on me and appreciate what I do for them, and that's a rich feeling no amount
of money can buy."

His eyes feverishly bright, Tom sat back, absently rubbing his upper arm.

Mark guessed what the man was up to. He waited until
Donna replaced the salad plates with their steaming shepherd's pies before replying. "If you're trying to sell me on
taking your job, I'll pass."

"Can't blame a man for trying. This smells so good, I'm
salivating like a Pavlovian dog."

Starving himself, Mark dug into his meal. It tasted every
bit as good as Donna had promised, and he swallowed several bites before pausing to comment. "This is delicious."

"What'd I tell you—Donna knows her stuff." Tom finished his mouthful. "Back to Stacy. She says she fell in love
with the good folks around here and the wide-open spaces.
The first thing she did after I hired her was buy a pretty little
house on the edge of town. I guess she was through waiting
for a husband to buy one with her. She's a shrewd one, that
Stacy. Efficient and sweet, too. She takes real good care of
me at the clinic."

Mark eyed the doctor. "Now you're trying to sell her."

The older man shrugged. "She's a fine woman, in need
of a good man."

"She'd probably be upset to hear you say that."

"So don't tell her."

Mark rolled his eyes. "You're right, though, Stacy's attractive. If she's as smart and sweet as you say, she'll find her own
boyfriend. I'm not in the market." After suffering through
two unhappy relationships in four years, both ending badly,

he wasn't interested in trying a third for a long time. "Besides, I'm on my way to L.A. I won't be back this way again."

"Not even for holidays?"

Mark shook his head. "I already told my mom that anytime she wants to visit, I'll send a plane ticket." If she wanted to move to L.A. someday, he'd help with that, too.

Suddenly Tom set down his fork. Sweat beaded his forehead, and his skin seemed more flushed than before.

Mark studied him. "Are you feeling okay?"

"A little peaked, actually. This was a long day." Tom gave a wan smile. "But then, when you're the only doctor in town, the days are always long."

"You're sweating and it's not overly warm in here. And you keep rubbing your arm." Mark checked Tom's pulse, then frowned. "You're in cardiac distress." For the second time that day, he pulled out his cell phone and dialed 911.

"I agree with your diagnosis."

Those were Tom's last words before he slumped in his chair and canted to the left.

"Tom!" Mark jumped up, catching the man before he hit the floor. Several diners had already gathered around. "He's having a heart attack. Clear a space around me," Mark ordered as he bent to tend the doctor. "An ambulance is on the way."

The next minutes passed in a blur, Mark doing CPR and awaiting the EMTs.

This time, he followed the ambulance all the way to the hospital.

"Come on, come on," Stacy muttered as she shrugged out of her cardigan and rode the interminably slow elevator to the cardiac floor. It was nearly 9:00 p.m. Visiting hours were over and she had the car to herself. She wouldn't be able to see Dr. Tom, but he was her boss and, more important, her friend. He was warm and kindhearted, the grandfather she'd always dreamed of. She wanted and needed to be here, and only wished she'd heard about his heart attack earlier.

She was worried sick about him, and also concerned about the clinic and the patients who knew and trusted both her and Dr. Tom. Stacy loved her work, which was never boring and paid decently. But with Dr. Tom's very life in danger…without a doctor to fill in for him, there was no clinic.

No clinic meant no job and no paycheck. She had enough savings to last several months, but she'd used the rest for a down payment on her house. She couldn't afford to be without work for long, and Saddlers Prairie wasn't exactly booming with employment opportunities.

But now was not the time to stress about her own future. Most important was Dr. Tom. Would he pull through? With all her heart, Stacy hoped so, because the alternative was too painful to contemplate. Squeezing her eyes shut, she murmured, "Please, please let him be okay."

The elevator pinged to a stop. The instant the door opened, Stacy rushed out. A good twenty people filled the waiting room, all of them Dr. Tom's patients and friends. Chattering in noisy confusion, they were loosely gathered around Mark. A good few inches taller and better-looking than any of the other men, he easily stood out.

As if he felt Stacy's gaze, he looked straight at her. His facial expression didn't change, but those eyes… As upset as Stacy was about Dr. Tom, and as uninterested as she assured herself she was in Mark, she still felt that intent stare clear to her toes.

Unnerved, she glanced away. Mark had no reason to care about Dr. Tom, and she half wished he wasn't here at the hospital. But he'd been with Dr. Tom during the heart attack, and had no doubt helped to calm both the older man and the others in the restaurant. As a doctor himself, he'd surely know Dr. Tom's prognosis. She worked her way toward him.

Men and women stepped aside for Stacy, touching her arm or patting her shoulder, offering more love and support than her own family ever had. The open warmth and strong sense of community were the main reasons she'd left L.A. for Saddlers Prairie.

Mark acknowledged her with a somber nod. Up close she saw the weariness in his eyes. His shirt was wrinkled, one of the tails untucked. Between Florence Jones and Dr. Tom, the man had had an extremely long and challenging day. All because he'd happened to be driving by the Saddlers Prairie exit. Stacy felt for him, but right now she had other concerns.

"What happened?" she asked breathlessly. "How's Dr. Tom?"

"We were in the middle of dinner, and he suffered an acute myocardial infarction—a heart—"

"Yes, I know," she interrupted, too impatient to let him finish. "But I don't know anything else."

"You're just in time to find out. I'm about to update everyone." Mark raised his voice. "If you'll all quiet down, I'll tell you what I just learned from the cardiologist on duty tonight."

An immediate hush fell over the room.

"Right now, Dr. Tom is holding his own. He could be here as long as a week and will need cardio-therapy, but the doctor is cautiously optimistic that he will make a full recovery."

A loud cheer filled the room. Stacy joined in, then promptly teared up.

"Provided he gets the rest he needs," Mark went on once the noise died down. "The nurses are asking everyone to please go home. They ask that you call before you come back, and make sure Dr. Tom is able to see visitors. Also, do not bring him food of any kind."

"You got it, Dr. Mark," someone called out.

People ambled toward the elevators, stopping to shake Mark's hand on the way.

Barb Franklin, the town's mayor and owner of Barb's Café, was first in line. "This one's a keeper," she told Stacy. "He saved two lives today—Florence's and Dr. Tom's."

The picture of modesty, Mark dipped his head. "Both times, all I did was contact 911."

"We all know you did a lot more than that, especially tonight."

Stacy hadn't heard anything about this. "What exactly did you do?" she asked.

"What anyone would've done—applied CPR until the EMTs took over."

"There's where you're wrong, Doc," Barb said. "Not everyone knows CPR, or could keep at it for such a long stretch of time. You didn't get a chance to finish your shepherd's pie. I want you to know you're welcome to come in anytime, and enjoy a dinner on us."

"Thanks," Mark said. "If I'm ever back this way, I'll take you up on that. Your food is outstanding."

Five minutes later, Stacy and Mark were the only two left in the waiting room.

"I keep forgetting to ask," Mark said. "Does Tom have any family we should contact?"

Stacy shook her head. "His wife died about ten years ago. They didn't have children. He always says the people of Saddlers Prairie are his family."

"That's too bad," Mark said.

"Not necessarily," Stacy murmured. "Having blood relatives is no guarantee of love and support."

"Believe me, I know." He yawned. "You should go on home and get some rest."

"So should you." Where would he sleep? Stacy frowned.

"We don't exactly have many motels around here. Do you have a place to stay tonight?"

"Tom offered me his guest room, but now… I don't know."

"He'd want you to stay there, regardless. He's that kind of man."

A middle-aged nurse pushed through the swinging doors and bustled toward them. "Dr. Engle, Dr. Sackett is asking for you."

"Me?" Mark looked taken aback. "Shouldn't he be resting?"

"He says he can't until he speaks with you."

"May I tag along?" Stacy said.

"Are you a family member?"

"No, but—"

The firm shake of the nurse's head and her stern expression silenced Stacy. "The doctor is too ill for visitors tonight," she said. "You'll have to check back tomorrow."

"I won't say a word, I swear. I just need to see for myself that…" Stacy's voice broke. "That he's alive."

Mark cupped her shoulder and gave a reassuring squeeze. His touch was warm and comforting, and she wanted his hand to stay there until she pulled herself together. All too soon, he moved away.

"It's okay," he told the nurse. "She's with me."

He made it sound as if they were a couple. Of course, they weren't—they'd just met—and they never would be. Yet Stacy couldn't help wondering what a romantic relationship with Dr. Mark Engle would be like.

Ridiculous to even go there. He was leaving tomorrow, and she was pretty certain that their values were worlds apart. Besides, for all she knew, he had a girlfriend who was probably waiting for him to make the fortune he so obviously intended to earn, then marry her. Just as she'd waited for Vince.

Mark was looking at her and she realized the nurse had okayed her to accompany him and was leading them to the nurses' station to check in.

"Thanks," she murmured once they made their way unescorted toward Dr. Tom's room.

"No problem. When I lost my grandma... I know how it feels when someone you care about gets sick."

Stacy gave him a sideways look, but his expression was blank. "I'm sorry," she said.

"It was a long time ago. But thanks."

She wanted to ask what had happened, but she didn't know him well enough.

"Is that why you became a doctor—your grandma?"

"Partly."

Mark didn't elaborate or volunteer any further information. They strode in silence down the polished linoleum floor, passing rooms where vigilant monitors tracked patients' vital signs with beeps and blinks.

Near the end of the hall, he pointed to an open door. "That's Tom's room." Pausing outside, he glanced at her. "Ready?"

No, but Stacy wouldn't admit that. She squared her shoulders, nodded and entered the room.

Chapter Three

Mark followed Stacy into the small room. The usual beige curtains were drawn over the window, and overhead, fluorescent ceiling lights blazed. He checked the monitors attached to Tom's chest, arm and wrist, and was pleased to see that the numbers were in the normal range.

As he and Stacy approached the bed, the old doctor opened his eyes. He was a big man, yet at the moment he looked small, weak and pale. Stacy stiffened in shock, and Mark heard her swallow thickly.

The urge to comfort her again grabbed hold of him, and as before, he cupped her shoulder. She gave him a grateful look, this afternoon's cold front forgotten.

Suddenly alert, Dr. Tom watched them with a canny expression.

Mark dropped his hand, and he and Stacy quickly stepped apart. "Your color looks much better than a few hours ago," he said.

"Thanks to your handiwork. Gol, I'm sore from all that CPR. Hello, Stacy. How'd you manage to slip in here?"

"We have Mark to thank for that." She gave a brave smile. "But I had to promise not to say or do anything, so pretend you don't see me."

"I don't see a thing. Do you, Mark?"

"Nope. You should know that, until a few minutes ago,

there was a whole group of people out there, pacing around and praying."

"I hope you told them I'm going to be okay."

Mark nodded. "Then I sent them home. They'll probably call tomorrow, hoping for permission to visit you and see for themselves."

"If I'm not too tired, I'll see them." Tom's eyes fluttered shut. "I'm sure tired now."

"We'll let you rest, then." Stacy leaned down and kissed the furrowed forehead.

Mark was touched. She seemed to really care for her boss, which was sweet.

Tom's eyes opened again, and he smiled at her. "I knew hiring you was a smart idea. Don't ever change, sweetheart, and don't ever settle for a man who doesn't deserve you."

Stacy flushed, but also looked pleased. "I won't."

"That's my girl." Tom's gaze sought Mark. "I need to talk to you, son."

"I'll wait outside," Stacy said.

"Stay. You should hear this." With two fingers, Tom beckoned Mark closer. "I know you're headed to that cushy job in L.A., and I hate to ask, but seeing as they're not letting me out of here for a while and I have a full week of patients scheduled, I don't have much choice. I need you to fill in for me."

It was the last thing Mark wanted to hear. He planned to leave Montana tomorrow and never look back. Hands up, he straightened and shook his head. "I can't. They're expecting me in L.A." Technically, not until a week from today, but if he wanted to give this job his best from the start, he needed time to settle in to his new apartment, buy a car and acquaint himself with the neighborhood.

Tom nodded against his pillow. "I understand, but look, I'm the only doctor in town. The nearest clinic is about a mile from where we are now, and we both know how far away that is from Saddlers Prairie. Who has time to make a fifty-mile round-trip drive, just to see a doctor? The good folks who use my clinic depend on it being there, and I can't let them down. I won't." Though his voice was raspy, he yelled that last part.

"For God's sake, Tom, do you want your heart to seize again? Calm down." Mark turned to Stacy, who shrugged helplessly. "Can't you find a temp?"

"I'm the doctor around here, and I'll choose my replacement," Tom insisted. "Besides, finding someone else'd take time, and you're already here. I'm asking you to work through Friday, Mark. Stay in my apartment and make yourself at home. There's a forty-six-inch flat-screen TV up there, satellite internet, and a top-notch wine collection at your disposal. Stacy knows where to find the spare key."

Her pretty blue eyes rounded hopefully—big and angelic, and enticing as hell. She had what Mark's grandma used to call a Clara Bow mouth—a plump lower lip and a sharp dip in the middle of the upper one. At the moment, her mouth was pursed in a silent, sexy plea that was difficult to ignore.

They both needed Mark. Like it or not—and he didn't— he was trapped. Settling in at his new place and buying that car would have to wait. He scrubbed the back of his neck. "All right, I'll stay."

Dr. Tom sighed, then closed his eyes.

Stacy let out a breath. "Thank you, Mark."

"But my job in L.A. starts next Monday, and I will leave Saturday morning," he warned them both. "Tom, I strongly recommend that you let Stacy find a doctor to take over your practice, so that you can retire and live another twenty years."

The old doctor didn't seem to hear him. He was already asleep.

STACY DIDN'T FEEL LIKE making small talk as she and Mark rode the elevator down to the lobby. She was still adjusting to the shocking changes in her boss. In the space of a few hours, the energetic doctor who was normally bigger than life had morphed into a frail, old man.

Standing on the opposite side of the elevator, Mark squinted at her. "You okay?"

"Not really. He looked *awful*." She shuddered. "Are you sure he'll be all right?"

"As long as he takes care of himself. He'll have to eat better, lose weight and exercise, but above all, he needs to retire. I don't know if he heard what I said, but if I were you, I'd take charge of finding a permanent replacement. In the meantime, hire a temp."

"He won't like that, but you're right. He's been looking himself for a while now." Stacy brushed her hair out of her eyes. "Between patients tomorrow, I'll send out more feelers. I'll talk to the mayor, too." Maybe Barb or one of her friends had some ideas.

The elevator pinged to a stop at the ground floor.

"Thank you for stepping up," she said as they crossed the silent lobby. "By agreeing to stay this week, you took a huge load off Dr. Tom's shoulders—and mine."

Mark muttered something about not having much choice. He was definitely unhappy about the change in plans. Stacy didn't blame him for wanting to get to L.A. and the lucrative lifestyle awaiting him there. After all, he'd never intended to visit Saddlers Prairie, let alone get stuck there.

The entrance door slid open and they stepped outside. Without the sun's warmth, the night air was cool, and she was glad she'd put her sweater back on.

Overhead, stars blanketed the black sky. Stacy never tired of the sight. She pointed upward. "Just look at that crescent moon."

"I've seen it a million times," Mark said. "I'm from a small Montana town myself."

"Well, you'd better enjoy the view while you can, because you won't see anything like this in L.A. Here's my car."

They stopped beside her red compact.

"Speaking of L.A., why did you leave?" Mark asked.

She saw no reason to hide the truth. "I went through a bad breakup, and decided I needed a change."

He looked puzzled. "You're telling me that you prefer a town that has exactly one real restaurant and not a single movie theater, museum or concert hall to the culture of a bustling city."

"Of course I miss those things, but I'd still rather live in Saddlers Prairie than anywhere else."

Mark shook his head, as if he thought she was crazy.

"The air here is always clean," she explained. "And we hardly have any crime, so I feel safe. Say I forget to lock the door to my house. That's okay—no one will go inside without an invitation. Around here, people look out for one another. If I need anything, I just pick up the phone and call someone, and a dozen people will offer a helping hand. You don't find that kind of tight-knit community in a big city."

"Thank God for that. Your community of friends are also nosey as hell."

"True, but so what? As long as I don't do anything mean or hateful, no one really cares how I live my life."

Mark snorted. "That's because you're blonde and pretty, and you probably haven't done anything to upset them."

He thought she was pretty? Stacy stowed the compliment in the back of her mind for another time. "You sound like a man who knows firsthand about upsetting people."

"Let's just say I come from a 'colorful' family."

His lips clamped shut, and she knew she wasn't going to hear any details. This was not a man who shared his personal stuff.

"You want colorful?" She gave a sarcastic huff. "My father

skipped out when I was two, and we haven't seen or heard from him since. Last year, my mom married husband number four, and she's already talking divorce. Oh, and I have an ex-stepbrother who's a cross-dresser, and twin ex-stepsisters who make their living telling fortunes, reading tarot cards and conducting séances. They're all in L.A."

Mark laughed. "Your family trumps mine, all right. But as you said, they're in L.A. Trust me, if they lived in the same town, people would look at you differently. You'd be an outcast."

What had happened to Mark to make him so jaded? "I doubt that," Stacy said. "So, is your girlfriend happy about your move?" She wanted to know if he was involved.

"I don't have one. Don't want one, either. My new job will be demanding, and the last thing I need is some woman nagging at me to spend more time with her."

Stacy's eyes widened at his bitter tone.

"That sounded harsh, didn't it." Mark rocked back on his heels. "The truth is, my last two girlfriends both accused me of spending too much time at the job. I'm a doctor—I work long hours. So yeah, I'm a little jaded."

If both women said the same thing about Mark's work habits, it was probably true. Developing a career was important, but he sounded like a workaholic, putting his career ahead of his relationships. More and more, he seemed like Vince—a good reminder that Stacy was not interested.

All the same she felt drawn to him. She firmly told herself she was glad that he was leaving on Saturday.

Worries about the future of the clinic flooded back. Saddlers Prairie Clinic had exactly a one-week reprieve before the lack of a doctor would force it to close. Dr. Tom would hate that. He might even decide to continue working, setting himself up for more serious health problems.

Stacy refused to let the man jeopardize his life any further. She *would* find a temporary replacement, a doctor willing to work at the clinic until she found someone to take over permanently.

"You're awfully quiet," Mark said.

Not about to share her anxieties with a driven man who could hardly wait to leave town, Stacy said, "It's been a long, emotional day, and we both need our rest."

Dead on her feet, she pulled a key chain from her purse, removed a silver key and handed it to Mark. "This fits the front and back doors of the clinic. Dr. Tom never locks his apartment. We open at eight-thirty. He usually wanders downstairs around eight, but you'll have to come down at seven forty-five and let me in."

Mark nodded, then reached out and tucked a stubborn lock of hair behind her ears. "That's been bothering me."

His thumb grazed her cheek, a brief, meaningless caress that warmed her all the same.

"It does that a lot," she said. "I should probably wear a clip, or maybe get bangs. But I always chicken out. Not about the clip—I'm just not sure I have a high enough forehead for bangs, and the styling experts always say you need that." Realizing she was babbling, she fell silent.

Mark's lips twitched, as if he were fighting a smile. "I like your hair the way it is."

"Thanks."

"You're welcome.

In the glow of the parking-lot lights, his eyes looked even darker than usual. Though Stacy couldn't read the expression in them, her heart thudded a little harder. She almost wished…

She wanted him to kiss her.

It seemed that Mark wanted the same thing. Tense and expectant, she leaned slightly forward.

A moment passed. Two. Despite the intensity of his gaze, he didn't make a move.

He wasn't going to kiss her after all.

How embarrassing. Grateful that he couldn't read her mind, and silently chastising herself for her attraction to him, Stacy turned away and unlocked the car. "Good night, Mark."

THE DIGITAL CLOCK BLARED rudely, jerking Mark from a deep sleep. Bleary-eyed and not sure where he was, he shut off the alarm, then stretched and glanced around. Blue curtains were pulled across the window, an area rug over an oak floor, a bookcase crammed with books. He was in Tom Sackett's spare bedroom, about to start his day as the acting doctor at Saddlers Prairie Clinic.

Scrubbing his eyes, Mark sat up and swung his legs over the bed.

After years of working long, crazy hours and perfecting the skill of catching a few z's anywhere, even standing up, he hadn't been able to fall asleep in this quiet, comfortable room.

Keyed up from the double emergencies and his own change of plans, he'd tossed and turned for quite a while.

Truth be told, he'd also spent considerable time thinking about Stacy Andrews. Looks aside—and she had those in spades—he genuinely liked her. As he padded toward the bathroom, he thought about last night. The warmth and sweetness Tom had talked about had shone through, softening and lighting her face from within, making her so lovely Mark could hardly keep his hands off her. Hadn't, when she'd needed comforting.

Later, as she'd stood in the quiet parking lot at the end of the evening, bathed in crisp night air and shadows cast by the perimeter lights, he'd wanted badly to kiss her. For a minute there, he'd thought she wanted the same thing.

Good thing neither of them had acted. He wasn't going to be around long enough to start something with Stacy. Besides, he'd meant what he told her—until he proved his worth at Archer Clinic, he wasn't about to start up with any woman who wanted more than casual dating.

He was still smarting from the breakup with Jill six months ago, a sorry experience that'd felt eerily similar to what had happened with Cara back when he was a resident. They'd both accused him of caring more about medicine than them, when he was doing the job he was trained for and working to build a career. He didn't want a girlfriend again, not for a long time.

There was no point in thinking or fantasizing about Stacy. Yet standing under the spray of the hot shower, he did just that. Imagined her soft, water-slick body pressed up close to his, her arms around his neck, her lips warm and yielding...

A certain part of his body stirred. "Don't do that," he ordered his body, the command echoing in the tiled stall.

Fooling around with Stacy was out. Period.

Some ten minutes later, dressed and ravenous, Mark stood in Tom's gadget-filled kitchen. How the old doctor had the time to use all this stuff was beyond him. The well-stocked fridge beckoned him to help himself, and soon Mark was sitting down to fried eggs, toast and bacon.

He was halfway through the meal when the clinic door buzzed downstairs. Stacy, and right on time.

Grabbing a piece of toast, he loped down the stairs, then opened the door.

A flawless blue sky backlit Stacy, her fine blond hair skittering across her face in the light morning breeze. In a lime-green dress and a woven, turquoise belt, with a matching shawl draped over her shoulders, she looked fresh and every bit as springlike as the new prairie grass in the field across the road.

She smiled, and like a bolt of lightning, desire smacked him hard. He pushed the unwanted feelings away and cleared his throat. "Good morning. Great dress."

"Thanks." She blushed, then noticed the toast. "You're still eating breakfast."

Mark nodded. "Left your key upstairs, too."

"Keep it." She hung her shawl on one of the coat hooks. "There's a spare in Dr. Tom's desk drawer. I'll use that until you leave. Go finish eating while I make coffee, print out your patient list for the day and pull the files."

"Coffee," Mark said. "I didn't find any in Tom's apartment, and I sure need it this morning."

"That's because he prefers tea. Did you have trouble sleeping last night?" she asked, shoving her purse into a desk drawer.

"Not once I settled in. The apartment is nicer than I expected."

"Dr. Tom likes his creature comforts. Not that he's at all wealthy." Her smile reflected her high regard for Tom. "He'd give the shirt off his back to someone in need."

The kind of man most people admired. Not Mark. "I'll take a big paycheck over a big heart anytime," he said.

Stacy raised one censuring eyebrow—how did she do that?—letting him know what she thought of his comment. Suddenly the air in the room felt a few degrees colder, just as it had yesterday afternoon.

Mark took the stairs to the apartment in a darker mood.

Chapter Four

Mark had just come out and acknowledged that he cared more about money than people. What kind of doctor admitted that?

The one who was here. Because of him, the clinic would remain open this week, and despite his skewed values, Stacy was grateful for that. If he wanted to center his life on money instead of people, that was his business.

Shaking her head, she headed into the kitchen. Using the gourmet blend again, she made the coffee. Mark deserved the high-end stuff.

She pulled two mugs from the cabinet. In the nine months since she'd worked there, she and Dr. Tom had slipped into the enjoyable habit of daily before-work chats. Over her coffee and his tea, they usually began with a review of the day's schedule, then moved to life in general. A sort of pep rally to kick-start the day.

She wasn't so sure about following the same routine with Mark. Still, she set out the napkins, sugar and a pitcher of milk on the café table for two.

She was sitting there, sipping her coffee, when she heard Mark hurrying down the stairs. Dr. Tom had a heavier tread and didn't take the steps as quickly.

He had a heart, though, whereas Mark was interested only in money.

Be nice, she told herself as he stepped through the door.

Somehow he made the little kitchen seem even smaller. Wearing dark pants, another crisp, blue oxford shirt and black lace-up shoes, he was dressed like any normal, nonranching male at work. Only, Mark looked better than most of the guys Stacy knew. His shoulders were broad, his belly was flat and his hips narrow.

She forced a smile. "You found the kitchen."

"Followed my nose. Sure smells good."

Mark filled the mug sitting by the coffeepot, then sat down across from her. His knees didn't quite touch hers, but almost, and she swore she felt the heat from them. In the cramped space the chairs were already as far apart as they could get, so she inched back in her seat.

She'd never had this problem with Dr. Tom, but then, Mark's legs were longer.

He didn't speak until after a noisy sip. "Now I can make it through the day. This is great coffee."

"I set the patient list on your, er, Dr. Tom's desk," she said. "If you want, I'll grab it and we'll review it together now. That's what Dr. Tom and I do."

"It'll keep. I thought I'd stop by and check on him after the clinic closes tonight. If we carpool, we'll save gas."

Mark had a point, but given Stacy's unwanted attraction to him, riding twenty-five miles in the same car seemed unwise. She gave an apologetic smile. "I have things to do at home and I can't stay at the hospital long. We should probably drive separately."

Mark shrugged. "Fine, but feel free to change your mind."

Stacy wouldn't. In the silence that followed, she sipped her coffee and mentally searched for something to talk about. Unfortunately, she couldn't think of a thing. She was too focused on Mark.

Uncomfortable, she stirred her coffee, though it didn't need stirring.

"Do you have—"

"Tom told me about your—"

They spoke at the same time, then both laughed, reducing the tension.

"Go ahead," Mark said.

"I was about to ask if you have any questions about the clinic."

"None at the moment. But if I do, I'll let you know."

Stacy nodded. "What were you going to say?"

"Tom mentioned that you bought yourself a house."

At last, something to talk about. This time her smile was genuine. "That's right. I've always wanted my own place, where I could set down roots. Now I have it."

"I've heard that in this part of Montana, housing prices are good."

"They are, and luckily I had enough money for a nice down payment."

During the six years she'd lived with Vince, waiting for him to make partner so that they could marry, she'd put away a good chunk of her paycheck as a future contribution to the down payment on a house. She hadn't minded, knowing that someday in the near future, she'd finally realize her dream of living in her own home with a husband and children. Ha.

"I'm planning to buy a house someday," Mark said after a moment.

"Let me guess—a big mansion."

At her mocking tone, his eyebrows shot up. "Maybe. What's with the sarcasm?"

Stacy told herself to apologize and keep her mouth shut. "I'm not saying I dislike money, because I don't," she said, forgetting that Mark's values were none of her business. "But it isn't the most important thing in my life."

"I'll keep that in mind," he said drily. "I see by your expression that you have more to say on the subject, so by all means, tell me what you believe *is* important."

She didn't have to stop and think about that. "Love, happiness and friendship, for starters."

"Without money, you can't *be* happy." Mark crossed his arms and sat back. "If you grew up poor, you'd understand."

"Believe me, I know about poor. You forget that my mother goes through husbands like water through a sieve. We never had much money."

"I'll bet you had enough to eat every day, and a place to live. Try being happy or finding love or friendship without that."

"You were homeless?"

Mark started to explain, but before he uttered a single word the front door opened, then shut with a loud click. He shrugged and hurriedly drained his mug, leaving his story untold and Stacy beyond curious, as well as more than a little empathetic. Talk about hardships. She probably should've kept her big mouth shut.

He glanced at his watch. "It's barely eight-fifteen. I thought we opened at eight-thirty."

"Sometimes people show up early." Stacy stood. "Shall we?"

With a nod, Mark rose, too, and pulled a small container of breath mints from his hip pocket. He offered Stacy one.

Peppermint, her favorite. "Thanks," she said.

As soon as they entered the waiting room, Bobby Wortham, a heavyset rancher in a work shirt, jeans and cowboy boots, limped toward them. He whipped off his cowboy hat and dipped his head toward Stacy. "How-do, Stacy."

"Hello, Bobby." She frowned. "What's wrong with your leg?"

"That's why I'm here without an appointment." Wincing, the rancher turned to Mark. "I heard about Dr. Tom's heart attack. You must be Dr. Mark. Got time to take a look at my ankle? One of my bulls kicked me good this morning."

Mark glanced Stacy's way. "Pull this man's chart, and when my eight-thirty comes in, tell them I'm running late."

A STEADY STREAM OF PATIENTS, both scheduled and walk-ins, kept Stacy busy all morning. Still, she managed to post ads on various websites. "Looking for a family doctor, temporary or permanent, to run the clinic in Saddlers Prairie, Montana." Time would tell whether anything came of her efforts. Later today, she'd contact a national physicians' temp agency and talk with a recruiter.

As usual, around noon things slowed down. Stacy poked her head into the office. Mark was sitting at the desk in his white lab coat, bent over a stack of patient files and scribbling notes just as Dr. Tom did.

Only, Dr. Tom was old and out of shape, while Mark could easily pass for a heartthrob actor playing a doctor in a movie. Simply watching him was a treat, and for a few seconds, Stacy did just that.

He looked up. "Come on in."

She was so focused on the man himself that for a moment she had no idea why she was standing at his door. "Thought I'd check and see how you're doing," she said after she entered the room.

"Finally catching my breath." He sat back in the swivel chair. "Is it always this busy?"

"Now and then we do have a slow hour or two, but being the only clinic around, and serving the outlying community, as well as the town, we're usually hopping. But we always try to close for lunch from twelve to one—unless something comes up. It's now a few minutes after noon, and if I were you, I'd take advantage of the lull, head upstairs and eat something. If you need me, I'll be outside, taking advantage of the beautiful weather."

"Enjoy," Mark said. "See you in about an hour."

In the little kitchen, Stacy pulled her sack lunch from the refrigerator. After work yesterday, she'd purchased several multicolor skeins of yarn for the baby blanket for Megan Dawson, and now she considered knitting instead of reading. But Megan wasn't due for over a month yet, and Stacy really wanted to find out what happened next in her book.

She spread an old quilt between the twin poplar trees out front. Leaning against the trunk of one, with her legs outstretched and her skirt hiked to midthigh so that she could get some color on her pale skin, she munched her sandwich and read.

The book was a fascinating story about a nurse during the Civil War. Yet as much as Stacy enjoyed it, she couldn't concentrate. Her thoughts strayed to this morning, and Mark's startling disclosure.

Not having a place to live as a child, or enough to eat—she couldn't get over that. The very idea made her heart ache for the little boy he once was. She also wanted details. Maybe he'd share his story over coffee tomorrow morning.

She was pulling an apple from her lunch bag when a clunky car chugged into the parking lot. She barely had time to stand and smooth her dress before a pair of lanky teenagers slunk out. Holding hands and wearing guilty, nervous expressions, they approached her.

"Ma'am?" the boy said.

She hated when people called her that. She was only thirty, not nearly old enough for the address. "What can I do for you?" she asked.

"Sarah Jane and I need to see the doctor." The boy's arm draped protectively around the girl's skinny shoulders, while she chewed gum furiously and pinned her gaze on the book Stacy had abandoned.

Whoever these kids were, they didn't have an appointment. "Dr. Mark is on his lunch break," she said. "Is it possible to come back later? If you'll step inside, I can schedule a better time."

"We can't come back," Sarah Jane said. "We both have after-school jobs. Lunch is the only time we can see the doctor, and we drove all the way over here from school. It's important," she added, flushing scarlet.

Fearing the girl might be pregnant, Stacy gestured the couple inside. "I'll check with Dr. Mark, and find out if he can see you now. Have a seat."

She hurried upstairs. Before she even knocked, Mark opened the door.

His lips lifted at the corners. "Let me guess—my one o'clock is here thirty minutes early," he said for her ears only. "Come in."

When Stacy stepped inside, he closed the door, probably to prevent the couple from eavesdropping. "I saw you sunning yourself out there." He gestured toward the living-room window. "You have great legs."

Stacy's face warmed, and she knew she was as red as the teenage girl downstairs. "You were *watching* me?"

"Not intentionally. I was looking at the excellent view."

His gaze flitted over her, making her acutely aware of her own body. Of him. Automatically, she sucked in her stomach.

"Pretty darned impressive," he murmured.

By the heat in his eyes, she knew he wasn't talking about the rolling prairie or the trees beyond.

He was attracted to her.

And the feeling was mutual.

Unwanted and already familiar reactions tingled inside her—warmth and a fluttery tension that was every bit as potent as last night. Then Stacy reminded herself—she wasn't supposed to be attracted to Mark Engle.

Why did she seem drawn to men with values so different from her own?

Too unnerved to meet Mark's gaze, she glanced over his shoulder. "There are two high school kids downstairs, a couple, and they don't have an appointment. They're on their lunch break, and say they can only talk to you now. They seem really nervous."

Suddenly all business, Mark drew his brows together. "Do you think the girl is pregnant?"

"That's exactly what I'm wondering. Will you see them?"

"Of course." He shoved the last of a sandwich into his mouth and washed it down with milk. On the way downstairs, he popped another breath mint.

"I'm Dr. Mark," he said, shaking each teen's hand. "Come into my office."

Stacy was pleased that he treated the young couple with the same deference as his adult patients.

The door shut firmly behind him.

She retrieved her things from outside, then folded the quilt and stowed it on the shelf in the closet. Sitting at her desk, she ate the apple. After about fifteen minutes, Mark accompanied the teens to the reception area. They seemed much more relaxed.

"Anytime you two have questions, feel free to call or stop in," he said.

The invitation reminded Stacy of Dr. Tom, and surprised her. Mark didn't seem the kind of man to encourage drop-ins—especially teenagers, who didn't have much money. But then, if and when these kids returned, Mark wouldn't be around.

She handed them each a card with the clinic's number.

"Thanks, Dr. Mark." The boy extended his hand.

Mark shook, then nodded. "You take care, Byron. You, too, Sarah Jane."

"Well?" Stacy asked after the door shut behind them.

"She isn't pregnant. Not yet, anyway. They haven't even had sex yet, but they're thinking about it."

Stacy certainly understood. She was no hormone-crazed teenager, but she thought about sex a lot, way more than she should. Probably because she hadn't had any in a good long while. "What did you tell them?"

"That they're smart for dropping by and seeking medical advice, that having sex is a big decision and there's no hurry and they should take their time. But that if they plan on making love, to wear a condom every time. I explained that I don't like to prescribe birth-control pills for teenagers, but if they're going to be sexually active, I will."

"And?"

"They agreed to think about my advice. We also discussed AIDS testing," he went on. "They're both virgins, but I advised them that should they move on to other partners, they'll need to get tested and request the same of their new partner."

"You were frank." Stacy admired Mark for that.

"Damned straight I was. When my kid brother was barely sixteen, he got a girl pregnant." Mark frowned. "That was a bad time. She couldn't tell her parents. They'd have put her out on the street."

"And yours?" Or had the family already been homeless?

"If my old man had known, he'd have rented her an apartment and paid her rent for the next year. He was always giving away his paycheck instead of using the money to take care of his own family."

"Was?" Stacy asked.

"He died when I was a sophomore in college."

"I'm sorry."

Mark scratched the back of his neck. "He was an alcoholic and had been sick for a while—cirrhosis of the liver. Anyway, when Kevin's girlfriend found out she was pregnant, our dad was on the road—he was a long-distance trucker. I used to pray that he didn't drink while he drove his rig."

So Mark had a brother, and a now-deceased alcoholic father who'd been gone much of the time and also gave away his money. Interesting to know. "What about your mom?" Stacy asked.

"She worked seventy hours a week, and was too tired to know or care."

In other words, Mark and his brother had basically grown up on their own. That didn't explain why, despite their mother working so much, they hadn't had enough to eat or a place to live. A subject for another time.

"Did the girl have the baby?" Stacy wondered.

Mark shook his head. "Eight weeks in, she miscarried. Lucky break."

"Did she and your brother stay together?"

"Nope. Think I'll go upstairs and brush my teeth before my one o'clock."

Her thoughts on Mark, Stacy freshened her makeup in the office bathroom. He may have grown up neglected and poor, but now he was a doctor. His mother must be proud.

No wonder money mattered so much to him. Still, by putting the almighty dollar first, he was missing out on some pretty special parts of life. He'd lost two girlfriends, and who knew what else.

Which of course was his choice, and reminded her that come Saturday he'd fly off to begin his lucrative position in L.A., leaving Saddlers Prairie Clinic without a doctor.

With just eight minutes before the one o'clock was due, Stacy had no time to waste. She picked up the phone and dialed the national physician's temp agency.

Chapter Five

When Stacy finally locked the clinic door and hung out the closed sign late Tuesday afternoon, Mark heaved a sigh of relief. After a full day working with her, he felt comfortable enough to flop onto a waiting-room chair.

As he stretched his legs out and rested his head against the wall, she put her hands on her hips, shook her head and smiled. "Just look at you. I'm tired, too. Today was *busy.*"

Despite her words, and despite working every bit as hard as him, she looked as cool and fresh as she had this morning. And she was still exuding energy. While Mark sat, drained, she emptied the trash, deposited stray magazines into the wall rack and drew the curtains.

She moved briskly yet gracefully, strands of her soft hair floating as if they couldn't quite keep up. Mark had never seen a hospital office manager tidy up, but then, when had he ever plunked down in a waiting-room chair at the end of the day?

The small clinic was vastly different from a hospital. Both were busy, but the hospital pace was more frenetic, the department manager urging doctors to quickly finish with the current patient and rush to the next. Here, Mark had been able to spend more time with each patient, explaining procedures and answering questions. A process he'd actually enjoyed. For a short-term gig, Saddlers Prairie Clinic wasn't half-bad.

Yawning, he stretched his arms wide. "I won't lie to you, Stace—I'm completely bushed."

A faint smile curled her lips, as if she liked the nickname. "Better get a good night's sleep then, because tomorrow should be even busier."

"You're kidding. What's happening tomorrow?"

"People want to meet the man who saved Dr. Tom's life."

"*That* again." Mark glanced at the acoustic tiles on the ceiling and shook his head. "As I said last night and repeated to every single patient I saw today, I did what any physician would do for someone in trouble."

"Don't be so modest, Doctor. You saved the life of one of the most valuable and beloved men in Saddlers Prairie. Around here, that makes you a hero."

In his two years at the hospital, Mark had earned the gratitude of numerous patients and their families, but nothing close to the adulation he'd received here. The abundant praise made him uncomfortable.

He straightened. "I'm no hero, and I don't belong on anyone's pedestal. I'm a man, period."

"A *heroic* man."

The respect and admiration shining from Stacy's eyes felt good. Mark soaked up her approving warmth like a wet dog in the sun. He wished she was sitting beside him instead of moving around the room. On the other hand, this way he could check out her shapely calves, the soft curves of her hips and breasts and the slender column of her neck without her ever guessing.

The phone rang, and he let out a weary groan. "Don't answer that."

"I have to." With an apologetic look, Stacy hurried to her desk and reached for the receiver. "Saddlers Prairie Medical Clinic. This is Stacy." After listening a few seconds, she held out the receiver. "It's for you—the mayor."

He pushed to his feet, trudged across the room and took the phone. "Hello, Mayor—Barb." He sat on the corner of Stacy's desk. "You'd like me to come to dinner tonight," he repeated for her benefit.

Her eyebrows rose, as if to say, *Aren't* you *special*.

"I appreciate the invite," Mark replied, "but I've already made plans to visit Tom this evening… He did, huh?" After Barb spoke again, he glanced at Stacy. "Hang on, and I'll ask her."

He covered the mouthpiece with his hand. "According to the mayor, Tom is exhausted. He requests peace and quiet tonight, no calls or visitors until tomorrow. Barb's hosting some kind of monthly dinner this evening that Tom usually attends. Apparently he suggested that I go in his place. I'm supposed to bring you with me."

"Me?" Stacy looked mildly surprised. "Are you sure?"

"That's what the mayor said. She also said to tell you that both Dawson brothers and their wives will be there." Mark recalled that Jenny Dawson had something to do with Stacy moving to the area.

"Really?" Stacy's expression brightened. "I haven't seen or talked to Jenny in over a week. The mayor likes to host these social events, but I've never been invited before. I wonder why Tom wants you there, and why I'm included?"

"Beats me, but if you come along we're sure to find out."

"Do you *want* to go?"

Mark shrugged. "I wouldn't mind, since I suddenly have nothing else to do. Besides, I need something to keep me awake a few more hours, and I'm too tired to go out running or flip through TV channels. But you have to come, too."

"And that would be because…?"

Unsure why he wanted her with him, he said, "The *mayor* invited you. Besides, you're the only other person I'll know. Mostly though, I'd enjoy your company."

Something warm kindled in her eyes before she glanced away. "Even after my little lecture on values this morning?"

"Hey, you're entitled to your opinion. The mayor's waiting."

"Okay," Stacy said. "I'll go."

Mark grinned, then told Barb. "They want us there in an hour," he said when the call ended.

"Good. That gives us time."

He eyed her. "For what?"

"A little chat with Dr. Tom. I want to know outright what's going on."

"You heard what Barb said. He's tired and doesn't want any calls tonight."

"By my definition, 'tonight' begins after the sun sets, around eight-thirty." Stacy gestured out the window, then checked her watch. "Right now, the sun is still good and bright, and it's just after six o'clock. If you pick up the phone in the office and I use the one on my desk, we can both get to the bottom of this."

STACY HUNG UP THE PHONE and waited for Mark to rejoin her in the waiting room.

"Tom sounds good, considering," he said.

"Much stronger than last night." Strong enough to be cagey. She shook her head. "I'm not so sure I buy his explanation about the mayor's dinner invitation. Sure, everyone wants you to feel welcome while you're here, but it's not like you're staying for a long time."

Mark looked thoughtful. "My hunch is that Tom wants me to get to know some of his friends. Maybe he thinks they'll convince me to stick around." His snort left no doubt of his opinion about that. "Thanks, but I've made other plans."

Stacy understood, but the truth was, she wanted the same thing as Dr. Tom. Already, Mark seemed to fit in at the clinic.

He handled walk-ins well, and the patients today had been pleased with his respectful treatment and willingness to answer their questions. He would make an excellent replacement for Dr. Tom, but it was all too clear that he wanted nothing more than to leave Saddlers Prairie.

No evening at the mayor's would change his mind. Given that and her own unwanted attraction to him, Stacy changed her mind about the invitation. "I think I'll skip that dinner and go home," she said, digging her purse and knitting out of the desk drawer. "I have a zillion things to do, and you don't really need me with you tonight."

"You can't back out now. Barb and Emilio expect you. Besides, I don't know where they live."

"I'll give you directions."

"Come on, Stace, go with me. Please?"

His gaze sought hers, dark as espresso and deeply penetrating, as if he could see into her and approved of what he found. The man was difficult to resist.

She'd known him only a little while, yet despite the huge differences in their values, she already liked him way too much. Against her better judgment, she nodded. "All right."

The slowly sinking afternoon sun was still bright. Outside, they both slipped on sunglasses. No longer able to see Mark's mesmerizing eyes, she somehow felt safer.

"Where exactly does the mayor live?" he asked as they headed for the parking lot.

"A good fifteen miles from here, on the west side of town."

"That's not exactly nearby."

"It really isn't that far, and I should know. I only live a few miles from Barb and Emilio, and I make the drive here every day."

"Why don't I follow you home, so you can get rid of your car, and I'll take us the rest of the way," Mark suggested.

Under the circumstances, she really ought to keep her distance. But driving from her house to Barb's would take, at most, ten to fifteen minutes, so what was the harm? "Good idea," she said.

Five minutes later, he followed her out of the parking lot and onto the highway. As usual, there were no other cars in sight.

He didn't crowd her, letting her set the pace. The sun was lower now, and vivid pink streaks spilled across the vast blue sky. On both sides of the road, the spring prairie grasses that grew greener by the day stood like slender sentries in the rolling meadows. The Montana air smelled clean and sweet.

As always, the wide-open spaces and magnificent colors awed Stacy. How could Mark ever want to trade such beauty for smoggy L.A.?

A scant twenty minutes later, she signaled, slowed and pulled onto Prairie Dog Lane. Hers was the last of half a dozen neatly kept houses scattered on either side of the narrow road, each on an acre of land. She pulled in a deep, satisfying breath.

Home. After living in apartments all her life, never for more than a year at a time, setting down roots felt good. Stacy loved her house, a two-bedroom bungalow Vince would have turned his nose up at.

He lived in a much larger, brand-new house with the woman he'd left her for. A mansion of sorts, just like Mark wanted someday.

Vince's wife, twenty-two-year-old Destiny, a college dropout with an ironic name, had recently given birth to a little girl. The newlyweds were blissfully happy. Or so Stacy had heard through the grapevine.

As always, whenever she thought about Vince and his happy little family, the world dimmed. But after more than a year, the once-searing pain had eased to a dull ache. That didn't make the feelings of loss and hurt any easier to bear.

"It doesn't matter," she told herself as she raised her chin. "I have the house I always wanted." But sadly, not the husband or baby—and no prospects in sight.

Would she ever meet the man of her dreams? Stacy didn't ask for much. Her ideal partner didn't have to be handsome, and his annual income didn't matter. She simply wanted a man who shared her longing to raise a child or two, then grow old with each other. With maybe a dog to keep ST on his toes.

Her driveway was a few yards ahead. For Mark's benefit, she signaled, then glanced in the rearview mirror. Behind her, he waved and smiled. Stacy's stomach fluttered, a potent reminder that her taste in men didn't always reflect her best interests.

On the heels of that thought, a panicky feeling knotted her stomach. Why in the world had she agreed to carpool with Mark tonight? Even if Barb did live close, keeping her distance was best.

Too late now. With a sigh, Stacy pushed the garage-door opener.

Not counting tonight, Mark was in town only three more days. For such a short time, she could weather anything. Then once he left, she'd forget all about him.

STACY'S ONE-AND-A-HALF-STORY bungalow was painted a soft yellow, with a dark green front door and shutters. Spring flowers on the verge of blooming filled the window boxes under the main-floor and upstairs windows, as well as the garden beds that stretched along both sides of the front door. Like all the other yards on the street, hers was well kept and huge.

A neat, modest house in a neat, modest neighborhood. Exactly the kind of place Mark had longed to live in both when his family had rented a dump in the tenements, and during the few awful months when he, Kevin and their mom had lived in the old Buick.

Stacy pulled into the garage. Seconds later, she ducked out again, just ahead of the closing automatic door. She held up a finger, then dashed up the steps of the house. She was inside a few minutes, before the drapes closed and the porch light flashed on. Carrying a knit shawl, she moved gracefully toward Mark's car.

He had no intention of physically touching her, but he could sure look. The slanting sunlight almost penetrated the skirt of her dress, showing seductive hints of thigh, and caressed her flyaway hair, turning the blond shade to burnished gold.

Did she have any idea what a desirable, beautiful woman she was?

Mark's body began to stir. Clamping a lid on his unwanted desire, he leaned across the passenger seat and opened the door. And decided Stacy's ex must be crazy for giving her up for a younger woman.

"Nice place," he said when she slid into the seat and closed her door.

"I like it." Sunglasses hid her eyes, but her mouth eased into a pleased smile, the bow in her upper lip stretching and flattening a fraction.

He wanted to kiss that sweet dip, then explore the corners of her mouth. Then slide over to a full lip press and go on from there...

Mark shifted in his seat and backed out of Stacy's driveway.

"Sorry to keep you waiting," she said. "I had to say hello to ST—that's my parrot—and explain that I'll be back later."

Mark chuckled. "Did he complain?"

"No, thank heavens."

Curious, he glanced at her.

"I found Smooth Talker from an ad on Craigslist. His owner, a marine, was about to deploy and wanted a good home for him. I didn't realize what a potty mouth the little fella has until the first time he was upset."

"I know nothing about parrots. What exactly upsets ST?"

"Mostly lack of attention. I promised him treats and quality playtime when I get home tonight. Drive back to the highway, then turn right."

Mark nodded. "Tom says you bought the house yourself."

"I don't exactly own it just yet," she corrected, "but when I pay off the mortgage in fourteen and a half years, I will."

"You're planning to stay here that long?"

She nodded. "I've always wanted to set down roots, and this is the perfect house. From the moment the Realtor turned onto this street and I saw the for-sale sign, I knew that bungalow had to be mine."

"I know exactly what you mean," he said. "I felt the same way about Old Blue—my first car. She was eighteen years old, a beat-up junk heap that barely ran, but it was love at first sight."

Why was he telling Stacy this? She was probably bored out of her mind.

"What kind of car was she?" she asked, looking more interested than bored.

"A 1974 Mustang II hatchback."

"Four-speed manual, with the 2.8-liter V-6 engine, or the 4-cylinder Pinto engine?"

"The V-6." Mark gaped at her. "How'd you know?"

"You won't believe this, but my ex-stepbrother, Stuart, the cross-dresser, bought the same car. I remember helping him tinker with it after school and on weekends."

"No kidding." Mark chuckled.

"Did you know anything about cars when you bought Old Blue?"

"Not a single thing. I didn't even know what a torque wrench was, but then I took an auto-mechanics class." The teacher, Mr. Madison, had taught Mark a lot about cars, and had encouraged him to go to college, rather than take a full-time job out of high school. "I drove Old Blue three years before she went to junkyard heaven right after my freshman year of college. What about you? Did Stuart let you drive his car?"

"I wish, but I was fourteen, and didn't have my learner's permit yet. He learned about cars the same way you did, then he taught me."

"He was lucky you wanted to learn. My brother was more into rodeo riding, drinking and girls than sticking his hands underneath the hood of a car."

"I'm sure you were just as interested in girls," Stacy said.

"I was." Though the girls he was attracted to pretty much ignored a skinny kid from the wrong side of the tracks. "But they weren't what you'd call a hobby."

"I know what you mean. After school, you'd find me replacing spark plugs and oil filters on the Mustang II."

Mark pictured Stacy peering beneath the open hood, a smudge of grease on her face, and smiled.

"What?" she asked.

"I'm trying to imagine you as a teenage grease monkey."

"That was the one drawback—getting the grease off my hands and clothes. But I really enjoyed the challenge of figuring out what to do, and what tools to use. Believe it or not, I found the process oddly relaxing."

"Exactly." Impressed, Mark looked at her. "Do you still work on cars?"

She shook her head. "Before the year was out, my mom divorced Stuart's dad. They moved across town, Stuart enrolled in a new high school, and that was that. Mom wouldn't let me touch her car, and I moved on to other things."

She smiled softly. "I haven't thought about that old Mustang for years now."

That smile probably lit up her eyes. Mark wanted to tug off her sunglasses and find out, but instead he kept both hands firmly on the wheel.

"I'd never have figured you for a mechanic," she said.

"Former mechanic. You, either." He liked that they'd once shared an interest in fixing old cars. "Where am I going?"

"Straight for another few miles, then you'll turn left."

He drove on, neither of them speaking, and thought more about Mr. Madison, who'd seen Mark's potential and had convinced him that his pipe dream of being a doctor someday could become a reality—provided he take the steps to make it happen. Mr. Madison had shown Mark the importance of setting a plan and course of action for his life, then using discipline and focus to achieve his goals. A plan that had worked perfectly so far, and had saved Mark from a dead-end job and a dead-end life.

Stacy was staring out her window.

"You're awfully quiet," he said.

"I was thinking about high school, my mom's divorce and the guys she dated afterward." No trace of that smile now.

"She dated a lot?"

"Continually. My mother can't survive without a man in her life. Whenever she brought home a new boyfriend, I'd head for my room and bury my nose in a book."

"Interesting. My mother is the opposite. My father died over ten years ago, and she hasn't dated anyone."

"She must've really loved him."

"Nope. She says she finally feels free."

Stacy angled her head at him. "I can't imagine having a mother that independent."

"Independent?" Mark snorted. "She's too broke for that."

"When you start your new job, you'll be able to help her."

"I might pay off some of her bills, but if I know Mom, she'll just accumulate more. She's never been good with money. Do I keep going straight?"

"Until we come to a fork in the highway, about half a mile from here. Take the left route. The house is a few miles down the road." Stacy's hands twisted in her lap. "If you want to know the truth, I'm a little nervous about tonight. I don't know Barb all that well."

"That makes two of us." The sun was lower now, and Mark removed his sunglasses.

"The food will be good," Stacy said, dropping her sunglasses into a case. "You probably know that Barb's husband, Emilio, is the chef at their restaurant."

"Yes, and the guy sure knows his way around a kitchen. I wonder who'll run the restaurant tonight."

"I'm not sure, but since they do this once a month, they must've worked it out."

"At least you know everyone—especially the Dawsons." Mark turned onto a narrow road.

"That is a plus. Jenny and I were roommates at the University of Washington, in Seattle. After we graduated, I moved to L.A. for a job, but we kept in touch. A few years ago, she came here to teach at the one-room school. Did you attend one of those?"

Mark shook his head. "Steer Bluff is too small for its own school. I rode a bus along with kids from several nearby towns."

"Ah. Anyway, one of Jenny's students was Abby Dawson, a cute little girl whose mother died shortly after she was born. Abby couldn't talk when she started school, but Jenny helped her. Then she and Adam—Abby's dad—fell in love. They're married now, and insanely happy."

Stacy let out an audible breath.

"That's one big sigh," Mark noted.

"I like the romance of it, you know?"

"You want the same thing to happen to you."

"Something like that. Doesn't everyone?"

"I'm in no hurry."

"That's right, you've had a couple of bad relationships and want to focus on your career."

She didn't sound sarcastic, but Mark wasn't sure. He shot her a wary look. Her expression was sweet, almost angelic. Too angelic. "Back in high school, I made a life plan for myself," he explained. "That plan is the reason I was able to become a doctor, and the reason I was hired for the position at Archer. What's wrong with that?"

"Planning is a good thing," she said. "But I was thinking that my ex was a lot like you."

"I doubt that. I wouldn't have done what he did."

"You mean, dump me for a younger model? I figured Dr. Tom told you. Everyone else knows—no reason why you shouldn't, too."

"I think your ex was crazy."

"Thanks, Mark. So do I."

He waited to hear more, but Stacy changed the subject.

"Back to tonight," she said. "I can't stay late, because I really do need to spend time with ST, and tackle a few chores around the house."

"We'll use that as an excuse to cut and run after dinner." He swiped his brow. "Now that we have an exit plan, I can relax."

She laughed, an infectious sound that coaxed out a smile of his own. "What's so funny?" he asked.

"You look so relieved about leaving early. Barb's house is straight ahead, on the corner."

Two other cars were parked in the U-shaped driveway. "The navy sedan belongs to Will and Carol Borden," Stacy said. "Will is the only CPA in town. Gabe and Louisa Bennett drive the SUV. He's the sheriff. Carol, Louisa, Jenny, her sister-in-law, Megan, and I are all members of the same book club."

"A book club—cool," Mark said. "I met Sheriff Bennett the other day."

"At Florence Jones's car accident—that's right. I don't see any of the Dawsons' cars, but I'm sure they'll be here soon."

Mark turned off the engine and pocketed the key. "Ready?"

Stacy nodded. They exited the car and headed for the front door.

Chapter Six

Feeling slightly out of place, Stacy stood sipping her wine in Barb and Emilio Franklin's living room, an airy space featuring a massive stone fireplace and interesting art. Delicious aromas floated from their professional chef's kitchen, making her mouth water, but no one else seemed to notice. They were too busy focusing on Mark.

As soon as Barb had welcomed them inside, the Franklins, the Bennetts and the Bordens had circled Mark like paparazzi around a celebrity. For all his talk about needing Stacy's company tonight, he seemed perfectly at ease in a group of relative strangers.

She could've stayed home, worked in the garden and played with ST. At least she wouldn't be here long. Two hours, tops, she guessed—provided Mark didn't change his mind and decide he wanted to stay longer.

If only she hadn't agreed to drive here with him. But then she wouldn't have learned more about his mother, or that he had once shared Stacy's interest in keeping old cars running. He wasn't at all what he'd first seemed.

"Earth to Stacy," Mark teased.

She forced a bright smile. "Sorry. I was thinking about our crazy day today."

"It was *really* busy," Mark said to the people gathered

around him. "Stacy's amazing. She knows how to run a smooth office."

Everyone smiled at her, as if she were a celebrity by association.

Happy that Mark had noticed her contribution to the clinic, Stacy also smiled. "I appreciate the compliment, Dr. Engle."

The doorbell chimed. Moments later, Barb ushered Jenny and Adam, Adam's brother, Drew, and his very pregnant wife, Megan, into the living room.

At last. As Emilio fixed drinks for the two couples, Stacy greeted Adam and Drew with a grin, then hugged her two friends.

"Mark, meet Adam and Drew Dawson and their wives, Jenny and Megan," Barb said as she introduced the two couples to Mark. "They run one of the most successful beef cattle ranches in eastern Montana."

Smiling broadly, Mark shook hands all around.

"We're relieved that you're filling in for Dr. Tom," Jenny said. "You should know that one of my students went home sick this afternoon with what looked like chicken pox. You'll probably hear from his mother sometime this evening."

"Thanks for the heads-up." Mark glanced at Megan. "How far along are you?"

"Thirty-four weeks."

"Boy or girl?"

"Drew and I don't know yet. We want to be surprised."

"They won't share the names they've picked out, either," Jenny said.

As usual, Jenny was radiant, and Adam wore an almost giddy expression of joy. Nothing new there—they were as gaga over each other now as they had been when they married two years ago. Still, Stacy sensed that something between them had shifted in a very positive way.

As soon as she could do so without being rude, she pulled

Jenny aside. "What's going on with you and Adam?" she murmured in a voice too low for other ears.

"You mean, dinner at the mayor's? It is pretty cool. This is the first time any of us has been invited."

"I'm not talking about tonight," Stacy said. "You and Adam seem *different*."

Jenny's lips twitched, as if she were dying to divulge a secret. "If you want to know why, stick around after our book-club meeting and I'll tell you." This Saturday's gathering was at the Dawson ranch. "In fact, why don't you plan on staying for dinner?"

That sounded like fun, and Stacy happily accepted. "I'd love to."

"Wonderful. Mark—wow, is he good-looking," Jenny said in a whisper. "Too bad he's leaving so soon. With Dr. Tom out, we need a doctor in this town."

Stacy agreed. "At least he's here through the week."

Emilio headed for the kitchen to check on dinner, and Barb refreshed the drinks, then gestured everyone to sit down in the living room. Stacy found a seat across the coffee table from Mark.

After passing the appetizer tray, Barb dragged an armchair over and squeezed in between Mark and the sheriff. "You've told us about your first day at the clinic," she said to Mark, "but not how you like Saddlers Prairie."

He gave Stacy a here-we-go look. "I've only been here twenty-four hours. Six of those were spent sleeping and roughly nine working, so that's hard to say."

"Ours is a wonderful town, nestled among some of the most beautiful countryside in the U.S. While you're here, I hope you'll take advantage of the opportunity to explore."

The mayor sounded like a tour guide desperate to sell a travel package. Stacy was embarrassed.

"With the clinic so busy and me only in town a few days, I doubt I'll have time," Mark said.

"You'll have your evenings," Barb countered. "This time of year, the sun doesn't set until nearly eight-thirty. And our Big Sky sunsets are spectacular. You really don't want to miss those. But of course, being from Steer Bluff, you already know that."

Apparently finished with her sales pitch, the mayor sat back and helped herself to an appetizer. Stacy released a tense breath.

"When do you leave for L.A., Mark?" Jenny asked.

He seemed grateful for the change of subject. "Saturday morning. The following Monday, I start my new job at Archer Clinic."

"What is Archer Clinic?" Louisa Bennett asked.

"A medical clinic on Rodeo Drive. The patients asked for a family-practice doctor to be on hand, and I'll be Archer's first. The clinic is set up as a partnership, and in five to seven years I hope to buy a stake in the business. This is a great opportunity for me."

"Rodeo Drive?" Carol Borden looked intrigued. "You'll probably meet celebrities."

Mark nodded, then answered a few more questions. "Archer is a state-of-the-art facility with all the latest diagnostic tools," he finished.

Barb stiffened, as if insulted. "Our clinic isn't exactly draconian."

"Actually, for a small-town clinic, it's very impressive," Mark agreed.

But sadly, not impressive enough for him. "That reminds me," Stacy said. "I phoned the national physician's temp agency today and told them we need a doctor, asap."

Mark looked surprised. "When did you find the time to make that call?"

"I *made* time. Hiring a replacement for Dr. Tom is too important to put off."

"We all know what happens if we don't find someone by the time Mark leaves town," Barb said, her gaze fastened on him.

Talk about putting the man on the spot. As much as Stacy wanted him to stay, she didn't approve of the mayor's pressure tactics.

Mark's eyes narrowed fractionally, a silent warning to Barb to back off. Still, the unflappable mayor opened her mouth, no doubt to put him on the spot again.

Stacy decided to change the subject. "We spoke to Dr. Tom just before we left the clinic tonight. He sounded much better, though he was tired. I'm planning to visit him after work tomorrow."

"Take Mark with you, Stacy," Barb said. "On the drive, be sure to point out our lovely—"

To Stacy's relief, Emilio cut his wife off by summoning everyone to dinner.

Barb directed her guests to various places around the ample dining-room table, Stacy across from Mark. Once they were seated, she realized that, except for her and Mark, everyone was part of a couple.

Was that why Barb had invited her—to make an even number around the table?

Emilio had prepared a delicious roast-beef dinner, and after numerous compliments, the dinner conversation turned to a local land issue. When a lull fell, Barb suddenly leaned forward, her gaze on Mark. "You'll no doubt earn a large salary at Archer Clinic."

Stacy gasped at the rude comment. Everyone else at the table seemed shocked into silence.

"That's my business," Mark all but growled.

Emilio eyed his wife. "Stop pestering the man, Barb."

"I only ask because I want to know what we're up against."

About to spear the last of his roast beef, Mark paused. "Excuse me?"

"Isn't it obvious? I want you to consider staying in Saddlers Prairie and running our clinic."

Mark's fork clattered against his plate. "Let me spell it out for you, Mayor. I already have a job in L.A., and I'm not interested." His voice was dangerously quiet. "So either drop the subject, or I'll leave right now."

Chastened at last, Barb shut her mouth. The rest of the meal passed uneventfully, though no one seemed particularly at ease. Mark certainly wasn't. His expression remained as tightly closed as Stacy's house shutters during a dust storm. She could hardly wait to leave.

During dessert and coffee, she caught Mark's eye and signaled that anytime he wanted to go, she was ready.

When Emilio offered seconds, Mark shook his head and pushed his chair back.

"I enjoyed meeting everyone, and thanks for a great meal, but Stacy needs to get home and so do I. Please don't get up. We'll see ourselves out."

GUIDED THROUGH THE DARKNESS by motion-detector lights, Mark helped Stacy slip her shawl over her shoulders, then walked with her toward the car.

"You were right about tonight," she said, pulling the wrap closer against the chilly night air. "Barb was unbelievably rude. I kept giving her dirty looks, but she was too busy pressuring you to notice. What a nerve."

She sounded outraged on Mark's behalf, which he appreciated. "She sure knows how to lean on a guy," he agreed.

"Without caring a whit for anyone else. No one enjoyed listening to her—even Emilio seemed uncomfortable. I can't wait to hear Jenny's opinion."

"She seems nice, and so does Adam." Mark opened the door for Stacy. "I liked Megan and Drew, too, and everyone else, and the food was outstanding. But for the rest of my stay in town, I think I'll steer clear of Barb."

"I would." Stacy slid into her seat, and Mark headed for the driver's side.

"She was relentless, but you stood your ground," she added as he started the car. "I admire that."

Mark nodded. "That woman is a barracuda."

"That's a perfect word for her. No wonder she's such an effective mayor. She digs in her heels until her opponents give up and wave a white flag." Stacy grimaced.

Even wearing the unpleasant expression, she was pretty. Better yet, she was on his side. More drawn to her than ever, Mark turned onto the utterly dark highway.

"Believe me," Stacy said, "Dr. Tom will hear about this tomorrow."

"From you and me both. Barb was right about one thing— we should visit him together."

His headlights pierced the black night, twin beams that bounced off the straight road.

"Okay," Stacy said. "Let's go as soon as we lock the clinic doors, before he gets too tired."

Mark smiled. "It's a deal. I'll drive."

"But it's my turn."

"I don't mind."

Rolling down the highway with Stacy beside him and no one else around felt comfortable and friendly. Intimate.

For that reason, Mark asked the question that had been on his mind since before Barb had brought up the subject. "What will you do if you don't hire a doctor to stand in for Tom?"

Stacy didn't even hesitate. "Keep your fingers crossed that doesn't happen, because then we'll have to shut down until we find someone." She stared out her window, though there was nothing but darkness.

Mark's conscience pricked, but why he felt responsible for a problem that wasn't his was anyone's guess. Regardless, he wasn't about to let the fact that Saddlers Prairie needed a doctor stop him from flying to L.A. and the great job awaiting him. Pushing the guilt aside, he said, "If I think of someone, I'll let you know."

"That'd be great."

The rest of the drive to Stacy's house passed in silence.

He pulled onto Prairie Dog Lane. Through the crack in his window, he heard a dog bark and a bird singing. "Do you hear that eastern meadowlark?" he said, braking to a stop in her driveway.

She nodded. "He must be searching for a mate."

Light spilled from under the drapes, making the bungalow look warm and inviting.

About to reach for the car door, she paused. "Thanks for driving me tonight, Mark."

"Thanks for coming with me. I owe you for sitting through that."

"At least we got a good meal out of it." Stacy yawned. "I could've used a second cup of coffee. I probably won't get to bed for another few hours, and I need the caffeine."

"If there was a Starbucks around here, we could order something to go," Mark said. "We'd have no problem if we were in L.A."

"Yes, but then you wouldn't hear that eastern meadowlark singing."

She had a point. "Is there any place in town to get coffee tonight?" he asked.

"We have two fast-food restaurants, but they close at nine." She glanced at her watch. "It's almost ten."

"I'll bet there are more to choose from near Flagg Memorial. After we visit Tom tomorrow evening, let me take you to dinner." He hadn't planned to ask her out, but wasn't sorry that he had.

"You don't have to do that, Mark."

"The heck I don't. I dragged you to Barb's tonight, and then I dragged you out before you got your second coffee."

"Believe me, I was ready to leave. I don't think I'll be able to look at Barb for a long time without wanting to slap her."

"I can just imagine you doing that."

In the ambient light from Stacy's porch, they smiled at each other.

Suddenly something shifted in the air, filling the car with a fine tension that buzzed through Mark and settled hotly in his belly.

Desire.

Their smiles faded at the same time, replaced by more serious expressions. He wanted to kiss her so badly, he could taste the sharp heat of his hunger for her.

From the responding warmth he saw in her eyes, she wanted the same thing. Yet rather than lean toward him, she opened her door. "See you tomorrow, Mark."

Letting her leave would be the smartest move. "I'll walk you to your door," he said instead.

"This is a safe neighborhood."

"I'll walk you, anyway."

Crisp night air washed over Mark but did nothing to cool the heat burning through him. They stood together on the porch, under the yellow overhead light.

"Here we are again," he said. "Saying good-night."

Unable to keep his hands off her, he tucked her hair behind her ears, just as he had last night. His fingers lightly traced the delicate shells.

Her lips parted a fraction, but her gaze was fixed on his chest, as if she were scared to look at him.

"Hey, Stace." Mark feathered her cheek with his thumb, then gently raised her chin so that she was forced to meet his gaze.

Her eyes were so dark with yearning, he almost fell to his knees. With unsteady fingers, he cupped her face in his hands. "I'm going to kiss you now."

In silent assent, she closed her eyes, her thick lashes dark against her pale skin.

He started gently, a brief brush of lips against lips. It wasn't nearly enough. Eager to taste her thoroughly, he kissed her again, this time passionately.

She let out a sigh and wrapped her arms around his neck. All softness and heat.

Mark pulled her closer and urged her lips apart. Slipped his tongue into her willing mouth for a long, tongue-tangled kiss that left his body hard and pulsing and his control in shreds.

He was ready to pull her through the door, where they'd have more privacy, when Stacy pulled back.

At the same moment a voice from inside the house yelled, "Stop that, you two-fisted shit bastard!"

What the hell? Mark put up both his hands.

"That's Smooth Talker," Stacy said. "He gets jealous of other men."

"You weren't kidding about his foul mouth," he said, shaking his head and grinning.

"I know." Her hair had fallen into her eyes, and she tucked it behind her ears again. Her face was flushed, and her lips moist and pink.

Desirable and sexy. Dangerous. Mark's erection strained his fly, demanding release. To keep from hauling her close again, he shoved his hands into his pants pockets.

As if she'd read his mind, she glanced nervously around. "Thank goodness for the trees between my house and the neighbor's."

Mark agreed, and silently thanked Smooth Talker for the pithy wake-up call. He prided himself on his control, but the second he'd kissed Stacy his mind had blanked, need obliterating rational thought. No telling what might have happened otherwise. At this very moment, he and Stacy might be in the house, naked.

He backed down the steps and cleared his throat. "I'll see you in the morning."

Turning away, he strode toward his car.

Chapter Seven

"Awk, I love you," Smooth Talker crooned as Stacy offered him a sunflower seed.

"I love you, too, ST," Stacy said. "Even if you do have a potty mouth."

Mark had driven off less than an hour ago, and she was still slightly dazed. And not just from those dizzying kisses.

She'd felt comfortable with him in the car tonight, as if they'd known each other a long time. Having learned more about him, and having watched him deal with Barb, she respected and liked him even more. She'd *wanted* him to kiss her.

Boy, had he followed through. His arms around her, the hard warmth of his body against hers had felt wonderful. And those kisses… Stacy hadn't been held or kissed in ages. Not like that.

She closed her eyes, remembering his smell—a hint of pine, and underneath that, his own unique scent.

Sliding her finger slowly across her lips, she relived the hungry press of his mouth, the swirl of his tongue over hers, his hoarse groan. The unmistakable hard jut of his erection against her stomach—

"Awk, feed ST, you two-fisted shit bastard," the parrot squawked.

"Not until you clean up your vocabulary," Stacy muttered. "Ask me nicely."

"Awk, feed ST."

"That's more like it." Stacy held out another sunflower seed and went right back to thinking of Mark.

His arms had stayed firmly around her, yet her nipples tingled and ached as if he'd touched and pleasured them. The man sure knew how to kiss.

She knew she was making a big mistake, but tonight she hadn't cared. She'd been too lost in the taste and feel of him, melting into each sizzling kiss, wanting to stay in his arms forever.

She'd broken the kiss because she'd wanted to make love with Mark—and she'd known him all of twenty-four-plus hours. Frowning and shaken, she brushed her hands together. "No more seeds tonight."

Losing herself so completely—so quickly—wasn't like her. Smooth Talker seemed to know that. Stacy stroked the bird's brilliant green head. Foul vocabulary aside, he deserved a reward for seeing to her well-being. On her next trip to Spenser's, she'd buy him a special treat. "You're a good boy, ST, but you've had your hour. Time for beddy-bye."

"Beddy-bye," the parrot mimicked.

He stepped from his perch in front of the living-room window onto her shoulder and allowed her to carry him to his cage. After shrouding the cage with its cover, Stacy headed for the bathroom.

Deep in thought, she brushed her teeth and changed into pajamas. At some point between leaving the clinic and standing on her porch tonight, the casual working relationship she'd shared with Mark had transformed into something very different. A fiery, reckless relationship of sorts, destined to end before it really had a chance to begin.

Stacy never participated in short-term, physical relationships. Never. Yet here she was, wanting more of Mark's kisses. She wanted caresses that made her shiver with pleasure—and more—regardless of the consequences. Catching a glimpse of her hungry reflection in the mirror over the sink, she bit her lip.

Was she out of her mind?

Wanting Mark Engle was a one-way street, dead-ending in heartbreak.

What am I going to do tomorrow? she wondered on the way to her bedroom.

She both dreaded facing Mark and looked forward to seeing him. Her feelings for him were more confusing than ever.

This was not good, not good at all.

Thoroughly rattled, Stacy climbed into bed and turned out the light. As she tossed and turned, she reminded herself that Mark was her temporary boss. He was here only three more days, during which time she would focus on running the office and finding a replacement. Nothing else.

Once he left town, she'd be able to breathe normally again. Meanwhile, she'd keep busy, and between her job, ST, the yard, reading and knitting, that was not a problem.

If all went well, no one would ever guess what had happened tonight.

MARK WOKE TO BIRDS SINGING in the gray predawn with a painful hard-on and a hunger for the woman who'd put it there. What the hell was his problem? More specifically, what had gotten into him last night?

He tossed the covers back and pounded toward the bathroom. If he'd kept his hands to himself, he wouldn't be in this sorry state. But no, throwing common sense aside, he'd kissed Stacy.

One little kiss, something friends might exchange, would've been okay, but the first touch of their lips had only fanned the fires. Especially when Stacy kissed him back. Her arms wrapped sweetly around his neck, her mouth eager under his, her soft body molded against him…

How could any red-blooded man resist *that?*

What was supposed to be a brief good-night kiss had turned into another and another and then one more, each longer and greedier.

Leaving him where he was right now—in bad need of release.

Muttering and wishing he had time for a run, he stepped into the icy shower. The whole cold-shower thing was a myth, but a guy had to try something to settle his body down. This morning, it was either shiver under icy water or resort to pleasuring himself.

Not much of a choice. Mark knew a far more pleasant way to ease his need, but he wasn't about to get involved with Stacy. Not today, not ever. He wasn't ready for what she wanted. Marriage and kids—someday, maybe, but not now.

Thank God he was here only a few more days.

THIRTY MINUTES LATER, EAGER to talk with Stacy and make sure there were no misunderstandings about last night, Mark took the stairs down two at a time.

She wasn't as early as yesterday. As the minutes ticked past, he began to wonder whether she'd show at all. She didn't strike him as the type to hide when something unexpected happened. Besides, wouldn't she call if she wasn't coming in?

Then what would he do? Mark paced the waiting room, which wasn't easy, thanks to the chairs and tables scattered around.

Finally he heard the sounds of footsteps on the walkway. Not wanting her to know he'd been waiting for her, he strode into the office. When the latch gave and the door opened, he ambled casually into the waiting room. "Morning, Stacy."

"Good morning," she replied.

A faint flush stained her cheeks, reminding him of her rosy skin after those kisses last night.

Mark's unwitting gaze swept over her. She was carrying a vase of flowers on the verge of blooming, probably from her garden. She *would* have to wear another dress that showed off her figure. This one was hot pink and fell to just above the knee, straight except where the fabric rounded her hips. She wore silver sandals with a little heel. Her toenails were blue, with tiny flowers painted on the big toes.

He really liked those toes.

As aloof as if nothing had happened between them last night, Stacy set the vase on the windowsill. That done, she briskly slipped her purse and a bag of knitting into the desk drawer. At least she wasn't shooting him a lovesick glance.

He should be relieved, but instead, he was… Mark couldn't figure out what he felt, other than an uncomfortable tightness in his gut.

"I'll start the coffee," she said. Bag lunch in hand, she pivoted toward the back hall and headed for the kitchen, the heels of her shoes clicking briskly over the tile.

Mentally scratching his head, he returned to the office, where he stayed until he smelled the coffee percolating. When he reached the kitchen, Stacy was standing at the counter, flipping through a health news bulletin that had arrived in yesterday's mail.

Looking everywhere but at him, she handed over the bulletin. "There's a piece about a chicken-pox outbreak in our area. You might want to read it while you wait for the coffee to finish. I'll go print out your schedule for the day and be back."

She blew past him like a cool wind. Or tried.

Mark reached for her hand to pull her back, but touching

her was out. He let his arm drop to his side. "Hold on a minute, Stacy. We need to talk about last night."

Back straight and chin high, she turned toward him and at last met his gaze. "I'm not in any particular hurry. I'm simply acting as the office manager I am. In other words, I'd like to pretend last night never happened."

Once again, she'd surprised him. "A guy doesn't forget something that—" *hot,* he wanted to say "—powerful," he substituted. "There's no way I can pretend it didn't happen."

With those words, Stacy sighed and lowered her chin, all signs of busyness gone. "It *was* pretty amazing. I don't usually do that—kiss someone I just met. Maybe a friendly little peck on the cheek, but not the kind of kisses we shared."

Mark hoped to hell not. "That's not my usual way, either. I want you to know that it won't happen again."

"No, it won't," she said with steely resolve. "In a few days, you'll be gone."

"Then we'll both put those kisses behind us."

"Why wait?" Stacy shrugged. "I think we should put them behind us *now.*"

The coffeemaker beeped, and she moved toward it.

"Good to know we're on the same page," Mark said.

"Yes, it is."

Her back was to him and he couldn't see her expression. As she reached for the mugs in the cabinet overhead, her skirt rode up, revealing a few tantalizing inches of the pale backs of her thighs.

Mark wanted badly to stroke his fingers over that creamy, smooth-looking skin. Swallowing, he curled his itchy hands at his sides. "We should probably skip dinner tonight and drive by ourselves to see Tom."

"You mean see him separately? I agree." Stacy filled the mugs, then passed one to Mark. "I'll go right after the clinic closes."

"Fine, and I'll grab dinner first."

"Perfect."

Unlike yesterday, Stacy ignored the table and remained standing. "I'll print that schedule now," she said, sounding crisp and professional again. Mug in hand, she exited the room.

That had gone better than expected. Blowing out a relieved breath, Mark took his coffee into the office.

Chapter Eight

Having filled in Dr. Tom about the outbreak of chicken pox, Stacy stifled a yawn and refreshed his water glass. Juggling the usual patients plus unscheduled visits from spotty kids—all the while pretending she wasn't lusting over Mark—had made for a long day.

The old doctor looked good, his complexion a ruddy pink instead of sickly gray, and his energy more evident than the other night. He seemed to be healing quickly, for which she was hugely relieved.

After a long pull from his straw, he settled against his pillows. "Why in the world didn't Mark come with you? He is coming?"

"Yes, but he had things to do first," Stacy replied, hoping her explanation was enough to ward off additional questions. "I need to get home before dark, so I can work on the garden."

Weeds seemed to spring up overnight, and the entire yard needed a good watering.

"Tell me about dinner last night," Dr. Tom said.

"Barb hasn't called?"

"She's got problems at the restaurant. You know Autumn Knowles, the part-time waitress who's worked there for years. Seems she ran off this afternoon with an agricultural rep who was passing through town." Dr. Tom shook his head. "That girl didn't give Barb one speck of notice. Now the restaurant is short a waitress, and poor Donna will have to pull double shifts. Good thing she had her knee surgery last year instead of this year."

"I'm sorry to hear that. What did Barb say about her dinner?"

"I want your perspective."

"All right, but you may not like it," she warned. "At first, the evening was pleasant enough, but then thanks to the mayor, everything changed—and not in a nice way."

The good doctor drew his gray eyebrows together. "What happened?"

"She kept pressuring Mark to stay in Saddlers Prairie, even after he asked her to stop. She made everyone uncomfortable. Not even Emilio's delicious food helped." Stacy gave her boss a dirty look. "The mayor owes Mark an apology, and so do you."

Dr. Tom made an offended sound. "I never told her to act like that. All I did was suggest that she make Mark feel welcome by inviting him—and you—to dinner in my place."

Stacy had her doubts. She was also curious. "That reminds me. Why exactly *was* I invited?"

"Because Mark knows you."

The innocent expression didn't fool her. "Baloney. What's the real reason?"

The doctor tried to stare her down, but Stacy meant business. At last, he waved his hand and gave up. "You know me too well."

"After working with you for nine months, I should." She crossed her arms. "I want the truth, Dr. Sackett, and I want it now."

"What happened to Dr. Tom?" he said, feigning hurt feelings. "The way you're talking to me, you'd never know that I pay your salary."

"A real bargain, given I'm the best office manager you've ever had, and you need me." Stacy eyed him. "Tell me."

"All right, all right. The truth is, you're an attractive woman. I thought if you and Mark went to that dinner together... I want you two to get to know each other better, so that you'll be able to convince him to stay."

Oh, she'd convinced him, all right. To run the other way.

If Dr. Tom had any inkling about last night's steamy kisses, he'd read her the riot act for unprofessional behavior. And she'd deserve it.

Avoiding his shrewd gaze, Stacy dipped her head. "Aside from the fact that I won't stoop to that, I wouldn't even know how."

"You're an attractive female—you know exactly what to do. You flirt, make him like you, and so on."

They'd already moved to the "so on" part, before slamming on the brakes. Stacy frowned at that lamebrained plan. "This isn't some 1940s movie."

Mark might like her, but he'd never agree to live in Saddlers Prairie. That suited her just fine. He was all wrong for her, and the sooner he left town, the better.

If she could just find a doctor willing to fill in at the clinic for a few months, until they hired someone permanent....

"See, this is why I didn't want to tell you," Dr. Tom said. "I knew you'd fight me."

"You're darned right, I will. Mark's here solely because you begged him to step in."

"I did no such thing."

"Yes, you did, and he's counting the minutes until he's on that plane to California. By Saturday night, he'll be in L.A., settling into his apartment and gearing up for his first day at Archer Clinic. That's where he wants to be, so why would you even want him here?"

The old doctor gave Stacy a sour look, letting her know

what he thought of that question. "He's doing a good job, isn't he?"

"Well, yes, but he doesn't want to stay here." Dr. Tom opened his mouth to speak, but Stacy wasn't finished. "You should know that I contacted the national physician's temp agency yesterday," she went on, bracing for a scolding.

To her surprise, he shrugged. "Probably a good idea— provided I interview any prospective candidate."

Stacy nodded. "I'll let any applicants know to expect a call from you."

"Any nibbles yet?"

"I only posted the ad yesterday." Stacy did her best to look unconcerned. "Sooner or later, someone is bound to apply. Let's hope we hear something this week."

Dr. Tom held up his crossed fingers. As grave as the situation was, he didn't look nearly as downcast or worried as she expected. In fact, he seemed quite cheerful, with an obstinate gleam in his eye.

Stacy gaped at him. "Don't tell me you're thinking about going back to work."

"Haven't decided yet."

"There's no decision to make. You plain out can't."

The stubborn man merely raised his bushy brows.

If he went back to the clinic, he could easily have another heart attack. "Don't even think about working again. We *will* find a temp," Stacy stated positively, both for her boss's benefit and hers. "I know it."

"We need to hire a new doctor."

"I know, but until we find that person, we'll make do with a temp."

Dr. Tom glanced at the wall clock. "It's almost eight o'clock. Another hour and I'll be ready to sleep. When did you say Mark was coming?"

"I'm sure he'll be here soon."

Time had flown by. If Stacy didn't leave right now, she might run into Mark—which she did not want to do. She was having a hard enough time keeping her mind off him. "I should go."

Just as she stood up to leave, Mark arrived.

STACY WAS THE LAST PERSON Mark wanted to see tonight. Avoiding her was his only reason for waiting until now to visit Tom. Out of sorts and tired of thinking about her, he silently swore and stopped short in the doorway.

She looked every bit as unhappy. "You're earlier than I expected," she accused.

Despite her frown and unwelcoming words, she was provocative as hell. Galled by his unwanted physical attraction for her, Mark backed away. "I'll come back later."

"You don't have to do that—I was just about to leave."

"Come on in, Mark," Tom called out.

Mark gave a slight nod and entered the room.

"I caught Dr. Tom up on the patients who visited the clinic the last two days," Stacy said. "You can fill him in on the medical details. Have fun, guys."

"Feel free to stay," Tom said.

Looking everywhere but at Mark, Stacy shook her head. "I really must get home."

Excellent. Mark relaxed. Now he could chat with Tom, then drive back to Saddlers Prairie and turn in early. After his long day, he needed a good night's rest.

"Go on, then," Tom said. "But you should know that the next time you visit, I'll likely be on the sixth floor, in the cardio-rehab wing." He snorted. "They want to make sure I have my strength back, when any fool can see I'm almost good as new."

His bravado didn't fool either of them, and over his head, Stacy shared a concerned look with Mark.

Tom definitely seemed better, and tests indicated that he was stabilized for now. But they both knew he was in bad shape, far weaker than normal. Mark doubted he'd regain his former strength for months yet.

As Stacy left, Tom gestured at the chair beside the bed. Sit down, Mark, and tell me about the past couple of days. How are you enjoying life at our clinic?"

"It's definitely interesting." The seat was still warm from Stacy's body, and Mark was mildly turned on—but then, every damn thing about her turned him on. "The on-duty cardiac nurse showed me your chart," he said. "You really are doing well."

"Course I am. Is the apartment comfortable enough for you?"

"Absolutely. I'm cleaning out your refrigerator, though. By the time I leave, it'll be pretty empty."

"That's fine. Most of the stuff in there is off my diet now, anyway. Stacy mentioned that you're doing a bang-up job with the patients."

"She said that?" Mark was gratified that she thought so. "Adequate," he corrected. "We've been pretty busy, and the work is more challenging than I guessed. Did she tell you about the chicken-pox outbreak?"

"Yes, and a good thing you agreed to fill in for me. I'd hate to think what would happen to those kids if their moms were forced to drive them all the way over here to see a doctor." Tom shook his head. "Some of those women don't have that kind of time or the extra money to spend on gas. Without you, they'd likely have stayed home, denying their kids the medical attention they needed."

Tom was only fractionally more subtle than Barb. Stifling the urge to roll his eyes, Mark let that one ride. "Stacy's put out feelers for a replacement."

"So she said. If we don't find a doctor to fill in when yo
leave, I'll have to go back to work."

"But that takes time, and I leave this Saturday," Mark re
minded him. "Only three days from now."

"No problem, I won't have to start back until the follow
ing Monday. By then I should feel pretty good."

Mark gaped at the pigheaded old doctor. "You do that, an
you'll die, probably within the year."

Tom started to cross his meaty arms over his chest the
winced. He was still bruised and sore from CPR. He glare
instead. "I won't leave my patients without a doctor. I won't."

Though Mark had suspected this was coming, the knowl
edge didn't make Tom's stubborn expression or his word
any easier to hear.

Either Mark stayed longer, or Tom cut his life short.

One hell of a choice, and he was trapped like a fox in
snare.

Making no secret of what he thought about the doctor'
emotional blackmail, he let out a string of foul words. Ton
endured stoically, waiting him out.

"Tell me you'll stay longer," he said.

Mark threw up his hands. "You win. I'll call my new bos
and ask for a later start date. I can't do any more than that."

STACY WAS COVERING ST's cage for the night when her phon
rang. The parrot let out a startled squawk. "It's okay," sh
soothed, then hurried to answer without checking the cal
display.

"Hello?" she said in a low voice as she moved to the bed
room and shut the door.

"Hi. It's Mark."

As if she didn't recognize that deep voice.

"You weren't in bed, were you?" he asked.

"Not yet." Suddenly the question registered—it was almos

ten-thirty. Panicky, she gripped the phone. "What's wrong? Is Dr. Tom all right?"

"Oh, he's fine, just fine." Sarcasm dripped from every word.

Relieved, Stacy flopped onto the bed. "But you're not. Let me guess—he pulled a 'Barb' on you."

"Made her look like an amateur."

Uh-oh. "What exactly did he say?"

"I think you know."

Mark thought she was in on Dr. Tom's pressure tactics? Insulted, Stacy huffed. "I have no idea what you're talking about."

"You don't know that he twisted my arm? Threatened me with going back to work Monday if you haven't found a replacement by then?"

"He did that? I don't believe it!"

"Believe it. You sure you didn't know about this?"

"I swear. Dr. Tom did hint that he hadn't made up his mind about coming back, but I told him he absolutely couldn't do that. Believe me, if I'd known he intended to start working again, I would've warned you. If he does that, he'll die."

"So I reminded him." Mark snorted. "As if that made any difference."

Resting her forehead in her hand, Stacy groaned. "Okay, first thing tomorrow I'll call the temp agency again. I'll offer a bonus if they find someone immediately." Dr. Tom would probably throw a fit, but too bad.

"It's worth a try, but I won't hold my breath."

Unfortunately, Mark was right. Stacy sighed. "What are we going to do?"

"You're going to put out the word everywhere you can think of, and do everything possible to find another doctor. And I'll continue at the clinic."

Certain she'd misheard, Stacy frowned. "You're staying in town?"

"Afraid so."

This was both good and bad news. The clinic would stay open, serving the patients as usual, but why couldn't Tom's replacement be someone other than Mark? Say, a woman or a happily married man?

"But you have a job waiting in L.A.," she said. "A great job where you'll make the kind of money you'll never earn here."

"You don't have to sell me on what I already know," Mark grumbled. "You also know how devious Tom can be. I don't want his death or the closure of Saddlers Prairie Clinic on my conscience. So I bothered my new boss at home tonight, which I didn't want to do, and explained the situation. He gave me another two weeks."

"You're telling me that instead of leaving in three days, you're staying two extra weeks?"

"Yep."

All that added time, pretending she wasn't interested in Mark, pretending indifference? Oh, great. Stacy wanted to argue with him, tell him to go ahead and leave. Unfortunately, that wasn't in anyone's best interest.

Her only hope was to recruit a new doctor as quickly as possible. Stacy crossed the fingers of both hands. Meanwhile, even if it killed her—and it just might—she'd continue to wear her office-manager hat around Mark and play the pleasant, efficient and dependable employee she was.

"Stacy?" he asked.

"I'm here. I'm sorry about the whole situation, Mark."

"Not your fault."

Through the phone, she heard a ping, then the slide of a door. "Where are you?"

"Just exiting the hospital elevator. I'm walking across the lobby on my way out."

"You're just leaving now? Then you must've told Dr. Tom you're staying. What did he say?"

"Not much. He smiled and thanked me, then said he wanted to go to sleep."

"My eye. I'll bet next month's salary that he's on the phone right now, spreading the news."

"Pleasant, efficient and dependable," Stacy murmured as she strode across the walkway to the clinic Thursday morning. Along with the sweetly scented spring air, she thought she also smelled coffee. She opened the door and sniffed. It was coffee.

Surprised—male or female, no boss of hers had ever taken the initiative to brew their own drink—she stowed her things, then headed for the kitchen.

Bent over the May edition of the monthly *Saddlers Prairie News,* Mark stood at the counter. Stacy admired his broad back and small, tight rear end.

Pleasant, efficient and dependable, she reminded herself, stifling a dreamy sigh. "Good morning," she said in her best office-manager voice. "You made coffee."

Turning toward her, Mark smiled. "Morning. Since I'm stuck here awhile longer, I figured it was only fair."

That he, the doctor in charge, even thought of fairness with his only employee—Stacy almost melted, the invisible office-manager hat she'd donned slipping to the side. She placed her lunch in the refrigerator.

"Took me a couple of tries before I figured out how to work this thing," he went on as the machine gurgled to a stop. "I wasn't sure how much coffee to add." He filled a mug and handed it to her.

"Thanks," she said. After fixing her coffee, she tasted it. "It's good, Mark. Nice and strong." She moved to the far side of the little room, so that the table stood between them.

"Not as tasty as yours, but not bad," he conceded.

His gaze linked with hers, and for one long, unguarded moment, they openly studied each other. Mark's appreciative expression soon shifted into something intent and warm, reminding Stacy of the other night, right before he'd kissed her.

Her nerves began to hum, and the invisible office-manager hat tumbled completely off her head. If not for the table between them and the mug clasped in her hand, she might easily have walked into his arms. Her knuckles stung from the heat, and lowering her eyes, she quickly placed the drink on the table.

Mark cleared his throat. "I, uh, I'll be in the office."

Stacy gave a brisk nod. "I'll print out the schedule and bring it to you shortly."

"I'd rather you didn't," he said in a brusque voice. As if he were angry. "When I'm ready, I'll come get it."

He left her standing in the kitchen with her mouth open. Had she done something to upset him?

It wasn't her, she decided, the *situation*. Mark was stuck here for two extra weeks, when he wanted to be in L.A. In his shoes, she'd be angry, too.

Stacy headed for the waiting room. The door to the office was closed, Mark's message loud and clear.

No problem. She phoned the temp agency and offered a bonus if they produced a suitable candidate within one week. Eager to earn the extra money, the recruiter, an efficient-sounding man named Wayne, vowed to find someone.

Stacy barely hung up before the phone rang. Though the office wasn't due to open for another twenty minutes, she answered anyway. "Saddlers Prairie Medical Clinic. This is Stacy."

"Hello, Stacy," said a friendly female voice. "This is Anita Eden. I need an appointment with Dr. Mark."

"Good morning, Anita. Don't tell me—Edgar and Julie have come down with the chicken pox."

"No, thank goodness. We all suffered through that years ago, and I am so glad we don't have to worry about this year's outbreak. This is an appointment for *me*."

"What seems to be the problem?" Stacy asked, as Dr. Tom had taught her to do with all patients who didn't automatically reveal the reason for the visit. His way of knowing what to expect. He'd also taught her that everything that happened in his clinic was confidential, to be shared with no one without the express, written permission of the patient.

"I, um… Hang on while I check to see where the kids are." Anita paused, then lowered her voice. "They're both dressing for school, so it's okay to talk. I, well, I'd rather not say. This is a personal matter."

Stacy just bet it was. The thirtysomething divorcée was a notorious flirt who at one time or another had chased after every eligible man in town. Or so Stacy had heard. For all she knew, Anita simply wanted to meet Mark and work her wiles.

She thought about telling the woman to save herself the effort—Dr. Mark Engle was here for only a couple weeks. A fact Stacy also needed to keep in mind. But Anita was a big gossip, and who knew how she'd twist Stacy's words. Besides, she was the only hairdresser in town, and Stacy was due for a trim.

"We're booked up today," she said pleasantly, "but I could squeeze you in first thing tomorrow morning."

"Perfect. I'll be able to see the doctor *and* open the salon on time."

No sooner had Stacy hung up when a young mother, worried that her infant son might've contracted chicken pox, called for an appointment.

The phone rang several more times. By eight-twenty, Stacy

had fielded no less than five calls, all of them turning into appointments.

A few minutes before the clinic officially opened, Mark at last emerged from the office.

"The phone sure has been ringing," he said as she handed him a copy of the schedule.

She nodded. "It's going to be another busy day."

Chapter Nine

Thanks to an extremely hectic Thursday, Mark barely saw Stacy except when she handed him a patient's file or he sought her out to schedule a test or follow-up. No time to catch a whiff of her flowery perfume, stare at those long legs or fantasize about getting her naked. After what had happened early this morning, that was for the best.

For a few minutes there, when she'd looked at him with longing, he'd wanted to get rid of their mugs and use the café table for something entirely different than sitting around.

Minimal interaction with Stacy was the way to go, and if tomorrow and the next two weeks flew by as fast as today, Mark figured he might just survive.

Keeping that in mind, on Friday morning he stayed upstairs for a good twenty minutes after he heard Stacy come in. When he finally came downstairs, she was at her desk with her cup. She flashed a smile as phony as his own. "Coffee's ready."

Mark headed for the kitchen. When he returned to the waiting room with his mug, she handed him the day's schedule.

"You should know that your first patient this morning is a notorious flirt," she said. "She may have made the appointment just to meet you."

He snorted in disbelief. "Nobody really does that, do they?"

"Anita Eden might. She wouldn't tell me anything about why she wanted to see you, just said, 'It's personal.'"

"Maybe she meant exactly that."

"Could be, but I'll bet you a week of making the coffee that I'm right."

She sounded pretty sure of herself. "You're on," Mark said. Just what he needed, some female patient all over him. He shook his head. "And thanks for the heads-up."

In the office, he shouldered into a clean lab coat. He was scanning the schedule when Stacy buzzed him on the intercom. "Your eight-thirty is here."

"Send her in," he said, bracing himself.

Wearing a short skirt and a skimpy blouse that showed plenty of cleavage, Anita Eden sashayed in. Her hair was jet-black and spiky, and heavy makeup added years to her age.

"Hello, Dr. Mark," she cooed, her perfume cloying. "I'm Anita Eden."

Stacy hadn't exaggerated. Ignoring fluttering eyelashes so long and thick they had to be fake, Mark gestured for her to sit down.

Twenty minutes later, any flirtation had vanished. Mark handed Anita a tissue and she dabbed at her eyes.

"Do you think it's cancer?" she asked.

The tiny lump on her right breast worried him, and he wasn't the type to sugarcoat bad news. "It could be, but I don't know," he said truthfully. "Sit a minute while I call the clinic near Flagg Memorial and see if I can get you in today for a mammogram and biopsy."

"Thanks, Dr. Mark," Anita said, looking like a frightened little girl.

WHEN STACY PUT THE CLOSED sign in the clinic window and shut the drapes at the end of a very long Friday, she was still in shock. "Poor Anita," she said as she put the magazines away. "How lucky you were able to get her in for the biopsy and mammogram this afternoon."

"With a little strong-arming." Mark handed her a stack of patient files. "The imaging department was booked solid."

"I guess I'll be making the coffee next week," Stacy said. "How long before you get the results?"

"I expect a call on Monday."

As bad as Stacy felt for Anita, she was also riddled with guilt. Why had she even suggested that the woman had scheduled an appointment simply to meet Mark? He no doubt thought her mean and petty.

"I shouldn't have said those things about Anita."

"I'm glad you warned me. She does come off as a flirt, but underneath the makeup and tight clothes is a very nice woman."

"She's also a decent hairstylist. This weekend is bound to be a long one for her."

"Some weekends are like that," Mark said.

Something in his expression, a slight tightening of his jaw and a sudden interest in the cuff of his lab coat, made Stacy wonder if his weekend would also be long. After all, he didn't live here and probably had nothing lined up.

She thought about inviting him to do something with her, but that wasn't the norm for an office manager and her boss, temporary or not. Besides, the last time they'd been together outside work, they'd ended up exchanging kisses she couldn't seem to forget. A dangerous experience she wasn't interested in repeating.

"What are your plans this weekend?" she asked as she pulled her purse and knitting from the desk.

"For starters, I'm going to relax. I'd planned to sleep in tomorrow, but Will Borden made a tee-time for seven-thirty."

"Will invited you to play golf?" Stacy shouldn't have been surprised. The two men had met at the mayor's house.

"With a couple of his buddies."

"That sounds fun—as long as no one pulls a 'Barb' on you."

Mark's mouth quirked. "They do and I'm gone. What's on your agenda tomorrow?"

"I'll visit Dr. Tom in the morning. I have a book-club meeting after lunch. We meet one Saturday a month, this time at the Dawson Ranch. And after the meeting, I'm invited to dinner with the whole family. By the way, they're as appalled at what happened at the mayor's as you and I are."

"I knew I liked them. Tell them hello."

"Will do."

Standing mere feet from her, Mark shrugged out of his lab coat, his straight shoulders hunching a moment. He opened a closet door and lobbed the coat into the laundry basket.

Oblivious of her warm admiration, he turned toward her again. "I'll probably stop at the hospital Sunday afternoon."

"I'm sure Dr. Tom will be glad to see you," Stacy said, relieved that this time she wouldn't run into Mark. With any luck, she wouldn't see him again until Monday, giving her a much-needed chance to get a grip on her intense feelings for him. She wasn't going to even *think* about him this weekend.

Yet she couldn't help wondering about his plans after his golf game. Maybe Will or one of the other golfers would invite him to dinner. As long as it wasn't a single woman. Stacy didn't like that idea at all.

Not that it was any of her business.

She swung the strap of her purse over her shoulder. Mark looked as if he wanted to say something, and she lingered at the door.

But he remained silent, and after an uncomfortable few seconds, cleared his throat. "It's getting late and I want to finish my patient notes before dinner."

Hint taken. Stacy opened the front door. "See you Monday," she said before she slipped out.

"THERE IS ONE MORE THING to discuss before we leave," Carol Borden said as the Saturday afternoon book-club meeting wound to a close. "We need to set a date for Megan's baby shower."

Stacy and the club's three other members were seated in the comfortable living room of the spacious house shared by Jenny and Adam and their daughter, Abby, and Megan and Drew.

"What's good for you, Megan?" Louisa Bennett asked. "Next Saturday? The Saturday after that?"

"Either one," Megan said. "I may look as big as a freezer, but I'm not due for another five weeks."

"You never know—Charlie arrived three days early," Carol said.

Louisa polished off the last of an oatmeal cookie. "Lucky you," she said. "Jonas was born ten days late."

Megan glanced proudly at her enormous belly. "At my last visit Dr. Tom said I'm right on schedule."

Stacy shot the three of them envious looks, then glanced at Jenny, who understood. Her mother, dead for over twenty years, had been schizophrenic. Fearing she might pass the gene to her offspring, Jenny had decided not to get pregnant. She'd adopted Adam's young daughter as her own, but Stacy knew she longed for another child.

Instead of sharing a sympathetic look with Stacy, Jenny gave a secretive smile, then glanced away. Making Stacy wonder.

"With Dr. Tom retiring, I guess I'll see Dr. Mark for my thirty-six-week appointment," Megan went on. "I just wish I wasn't so huge."

"Because he's so handsome?" Louisa teased, smiling.

Megan nodded. "Not that I'm interested, of course, but that is one attractive man." She gave Stacy a sideways look. "What kind of boss is he?"

"Not bad," Stacy replied. If you didn't count her strong attraction to him or the fact that she had to work hard to hide it. But she didn't want to talk about Mark. "When would you like to have the shower, Megan?" she asked.

"How about the Saturday following my doctor's appointment?"

Everyone checked their calendars. "That's Memorial Day weekend," Stacy said.

"I don't have a problem with that," Megan said. "I'm too pregnant to do much."

Luckily, no one had plans that Saturday afternoon. "I'll host," Stacy offered, already anticipating the party. "If you don't mind Smooth Talker's mouth."

"I'll bet he'll behave if we offer him treats and make a fuss over him," Jenny said.

Stacy shrugged. "One can hope. I'll make sure to have plenty of bird treats on hand."

The housekeeper didn't work weekends. By the time Carol and Louisa left, it was time to fix dinner. Ordering Megan to prop up her feet and relax, Jenny and Stacy prepared the meal.

"This reminds me of all those nights in college, when we cooked dinner together," Stacy said as she put the salad together. The Dawsons' kitchen was about three times the size of their little apartment kitchen. "It's been too long since we've done this, and too long since we've talked."

Busy at the stove, Jenny looked wistful. "I know, and we have so much catching up to—"

Suddenly the door to the mudroom burst open. All smiles, seven-year-old Abby rushed inside, followed by Adam and Drew.

Jenny asked Abby to set the table. Between the pre-meal hustle and bustle and dinner itself, the next few hours sped by. At the end of the noisy, laughter-filled meal around the big kitchen table, Adam shooed away everyone but Drew.

"My brother and I will clean up tonight, before we do our last chores of the evening. Until then, you ladies are on your own. Then it's Saturday-night movie time."

"Tell me when, and I'll make the popcorn." Jenny kissed her husband. "Thanks for giving Stacy and me time alone, sweetie."

"I'm gonna put my feet up again—after another pit stop." Megan waddled toward the bathroom.

"Will you watch me swing?" Abby asked.

Jenny smiled. "We'd love to, sweetie, but Stacy and I also want to talk. We'll sit on the porch and watch you from there."

"Okay." The little girl skipped ahead.

"She's so cute," Stacy said. "You'd never know she didn't speak a word until she was five."

"I still marvel over that," Jenny said as they followed Abby through the front door. They crossed the wraparound porch to the side yard, where Adam had hung a swing.

Minutes later, they were settled in twin wicker rockers, enjoying the darkening sky and unusually warm evening, and watching Abby's coppery red pigtails fly.

Jez, the family's large black cat, who adored the little girl, sat near the swing set, her attention on Abby, her tail twitching. In the distance beyond the fenced yard, pastured cattle grazed placidly on emerald spring grass.

"I stopped by the hospital to see Dr. Tom this morning," Stacy said.

"How is he?"

"Improving every day. Yesterday, his doctor moved him to the cardio-rehab wing."

"I'll bet he hates that."

Remembering his long litany of complaints—the physical therapists worked him too hard and fed him too little—Stacy nodded. "But he needs the rehab, and the work they make him do keeps his mind off the clinic."

"He must be relieved that Mark's staying a few more weeks."

"Relieved? He's ecstatic." Stacy hoped he didn't act as gleeful when Mark visited tomorrow. It would be like rubbing salt in a cut.

"I can't quite believe Mark agreed to stay," Jenny went on. "He's so excited about his new job."

"He's only doing it because Dr. Tom made noises about going back to work if Mark didn't stay."

"I still think he's a great guy. Are there any potential replacements?"

"Not yet." Stacy explained about the bonus she'd offered and the eager recruiter who'd all but promised results. "With any luck, I'll hear something early next week."

"For Mark's sake, I hope you do." Jenny called out something to Abby, then changed the subject. "I heard about Anita Eden," she said in a lower voice, the chair creaking as she pushed the rocker with her foot. "Breast cancer. That's so scary."

"We won't know for sure that it *is* cancer until the test results come back on Monday." Honoring the code of confidentiality, Stacy hadn't told a soul about Anita. She was certain Mark hadn't, either. She frowned. "How did you find out?"

"Anita told me when she trimmed my hair this morning. I heard all about the mammogram and her biopsy at the Flagg Clinic. Then when I stopped at the post office to mail something after my haircut, I found out that Val Mason also knew. According to her, Anita has been telling everyone."

Stacy shook her head. "I'm not sure I'd do that until I got the test results."

"You know Anita—she likes to share her life with whoever will listen."

"You're right. How did she seem today?" Stacy asked.

"As you can imagine, she was tearful, really worried and distracted. I'm lucky she didn't butcher my hair. She wasn't so upset that she didn't sing Mark's praises, though. To quote her, 'He's a terrific doctor, and a living doll.' I'd have to agree."

"That makes three of us." With a sigh, Stacy pushed the rocker.

Jenny stared hard at her. "You like him."

"Too much," Stacy admitted.

"Hey, if I were single, *I'd* have a huge crush on the man."

Unable to keep anything from her best friend, Stacy told Jenny what had happened after Mark drove her home the night of the mayor's dinner.

"Wow," Jenny said. "He moves fast."

"I wanted him to kiss me. But now I wish he hadn't."

"Because he's leaving?"

"That, and because he's a lot like Vince," Stacy said.

"Even Vince fell in love."

When Stacy winced, Jenny bit her lip. "That came out wrong."

"But it's true." Stacy rubbed her arms. "I don't think Vince ever really loved me. Or if he did, he fell out of love long before he ended the relationship."

"I think you did, too. I remember one four-day weekend when I flew down for a visit. At the time, you and Vince had been living together for about three years. You didn't seem happy."

Stacy ruminated on that. "Vince and I had our share of fun, but you're right. I was unhappy a lot of the time, especially those last few years. Mostly because I wanted to get married, and he didn't."

At least, that's what Stacy had always told herself. Looking back, she wondered if Jenny was right, that her unhappiness stemmed from knowing deep down that she didn't love Vince.

"Be thankful he's out of your life," Jenny said. "You weren't right for each other, and the marriage would never have lasted."

"I wish I'd realized that sooner, instead of wasting six whole years on the wrong guy. Seven, if you count the year we dated before we got engaged."

"Things happen for a reason."

"Really? Because I sure can't think of a single thing that justifies getting my heart broken."

"Maybe you needed the clarity that came with the pain— about the kind of man you really want, and the kind you don't."

Stacy definitely had that clarity now. She wanted a man who valued relationships over the almighty dollar. Which was why her attraction to Mark was so difficult to fathom.

For long moments, the silence was broken only by the twin rockers creaking over the wood planking, and Abby's voice, rising in song as the swing arced back and forth.

"Sometimes I wonder if I'll ever meet my Mr. Right," Stacy mused after a while.

"I never thought I would, either, and just look at me now."

Jenny fingered her wedding ring, a smile lighting her whole face. "If it happened to me, it can happen to you. Don't give up, Stacy. You'll find your Mr. Right. I know it."

In the growing darkness, the motion-detector lights flashed on. Somewhere an owl hooted. A pair of grouse sailed past the porch, on their way to roost for the night.

"What's Mark doing this weekend?" Jenny asked.

"He played golf with Will Borden and some of Will's friends today, and he mentioned visiting Dr. Tom tomorrow."

"What about tonight?"

"I didn't ask, and he didn't say."

"I'll bet he ate dinner alone. Shoot, we could've invited him here."

Stacy thought about sharing the Dawson family meal with Mark, pretending she wasn't interested in him while at the same time having to watch Jenny and Adam glow with love, and Drew treat Megan with adoring tenderness. No, thank you.

"I hope he's not sitting in Tom's apartment all by his lonesome," Jenny went on. "He could be, you know. There isn't much to do around here Saturday nights, and he doesn't know many people."

"You'd be surprised at how many people Mark's met. Someone probably invited him to dinner. If not, he's a resourceful man. He'll figure out something to do."

"I'm sure he'll tell you all about it Monday morning."

Stacy and Dr. Tom had often discussed their weekend activities. With Mark, who knew? He might stay upstairs until just before the clinic opened, as he had yesterday. Stacy suspected he'd been avoiding her, which suited her just fine.

Suddenly for no reason at all, Jenny laughed softly.

"What's so funny?"

"Oh, nothing." Jenny shook her head.

"You've been wearing that secretive smile since dinner at Barb's," Stacy commented. "If I know you, that means a big something."

"Well…" Jenny glanced around, as if checking to make sure no one was within listening distance. After casting an eye at Abby, who was sitting on the ground, playing with Jez, she leaned toward Stacy. "I really shouldn't say anything, but I need to share the good news with my best friend. If I tell you, will you promise not to say anything to anyone just yet?"

Stacy made an X over her heart. "You know I won't."

After beckoning Stacy closer, Jenny lowered her voice. "The packet I mailed at the post office today was an application to adopt a baby."

"That explains all those Mona Lisa smiles," Stacy said. "Wow. Congratulations." She and Jenny grinned at each other. "Tell me more. Any idea when you'll get this baby?"

"No, but we hope it won't take long."

Footsteps announced Adam, who joined them on the porch. "Ready to make popcorn for the movie, honey?"

"I sure am. You're welcome to stay, Stacy."

The family needed its privacy. Stacy shook her head.

"I'll go set up the movie. Come on in, Abby," Adam called out. "See you another time, Stacy."

After Stacy said good-night to Abby, and the girl joined her father, Jenny walked Stacy to her car. They hugged each other.

"It was so good to see you," Stacy said.

"Really good. We have to get together again soon and plan the shower."

"Definitely." Stacy lowered her voice. "When the time comes, I also want to host *your* baby shower."

"I'd like that."

Smiling, Stacy honked and headed down the Dawsons'

long driveway. She thought about the anticipated babies. First Megan, now Jenny.

As thrilled as Stacy was for both of them, she was also envious of her best friend. Jenny had found the love of her life, a man who adored her and would do just about anything to make her happy. Stacy wanted that kind of love. She also wanted a baby.

For now, she'd have to be content watching the wonderful Dawson family grow.

Chapter Ten

After playing eighteen holes of golf Saturday, Mark headed for Spenser's General Store to pick up groceries and something to read. He wasn't the only one shopping late in the day—the place was filled with people.

Patients he'd met nodded hello or stopped to chat. Val Mason, a middle-aged woman who ran the post office and had come in on Thursday with elbow pain, introduced him to her husband, Silas.

"My wife is so pleased with the exercises you gave her for her elbow," Silas said, pulling on suspenders that bowed over his big belly.

"I got Silas doing them, too." Val's apple cheeks rounded in a smile.

"And my elbows don't even hurt." Silas guffawed. "Say, Val and I are barbecuing ribs tomorrow at our place. Why don't you come to Sunday dinner?"

"What a fine idea, Silas," Val said. "You won't be sorry, Dr. Mark—Silas makes a killer barbecue sauce. Bring something to drink and come on over around six."

Pleased to have something to do the following evening, Mark readily accepted the invitation.

Tonight still loomed ahead, though. Too bad there wasn't a theater in town.

Not about to hang around the apartment by himself, and

damned if he'd set foot in Barb's Café, Mark quickly made plans. He'd drop off the groceries, drive to another town and take himself out to dinner and a movie.

"Where's the nearest movie theater around here?" he asked Val and Silas.

"Well…" Val thought a moment. "Not very close. How far would you guess, Silas?"

"Forty or so miles west of here."

Too far to drive for a film. Okay. He would cook himself a steak, then kick back and watch Tom's big-screen TV. A relaxing Saturday evening by himself. Big whoop, but it wouldn't be the first time.

On the floor of the old doctor's pantry, he found a hibachi and a half-full bag of charcoal briquettes. He carried both out front, setting up the barbecue between the trees where Stacy had lunched that first day, her skirt hiked up and her long legs outstretched.

She had the sexiest legs….

But Mark wasn't going to think about her now.

He set a match to the coals. While waiting for them to burn down, he headed upstairs again and called his mom to let her know about his temporary stay in Saddlers Prairie. Then he tossed a potato in the oven, made a salad and popped the cork on a bottle of cabernet sauvignon that had to cost at least fifty dollars. Tom had said to help himself. Besides, he *owed* Mark. Standing in the kitchen, Mark raised the glass. "Here's to a mellow night."

The cab tasted rich and smooth, primo stuff. Wine this good should be shared. If Stacy were with him now, she'd probably love this.

Yeah, right. She'd be lucky to finish the glass before he set it aside and kissed her. If the chemistry was anywhere as hot as last time, they'd end up in bed.

Tangled together, skin to skin, tasting and touching…

Bad idea. Neither of them wanted to go that route, and they wouldn't. Ever.

Lucky that he excelled at self-control. Yes, his control had fallen by the wayside the other night, but that wouldn't happen again.

At this very minute, she was at the Dawsons', probably having a great time. For sure, she wasn't thinking about him.

Mark wouldn't think of her, either. But he did. He imagined pushing deep into her slick heat, both of them crazed with need. Her thighs tight around his hips, her hands gripping his butt... His erection throbbed, joining in the fantasy.

Scowling, he plunked the raw T-bone on a plate and headed downstairs. The sizzling steak and mouthwatering aroma kept his mind on dinner, and his body soon cooled down. When the steak was grilled to perfection, he returned to the apartment. Sitting at Tom's kitchen table, he forked into his simple meal, polishing off everything in a short time. He washed the food down with a second glass of wine.

Then he stood at the window, watching the sun sink lower. The vivid red-and-orange streaks that colored the fading blue of the sky entertained him for a while before he tired of the view.

Now what?

The old doctor owned a large collection of DVDs. With no movie theater around, that made sense. Mark sorted through the selection, settling on an early James Bond film.

About the time the credits rolled, he downed the last of the wine. It was just after nine o'clock.

Too antsy to sit around, he considered going for a run, which he did at least twice a week, though not since he'd been here. Still full and slightly drunk, he dismissed that idea. He would walk instead.

He laced up his sneakers. Moments later, he locked the

door and headed up the road without any idea where he was going.

Except for the office and the handful of small ranches scattered around, there were no buildings out here. The only illumination came from the clinic's floodlights and the full moon.

Before long, he was well out of range of the clinic. Nothing out here but quickly darkening sky and prairie grass. And a deep silence.

Moonlight painted everything silver—the grass undulating in the gentle wind, the surface of the road. The world looked magical, romantic.

Lonely.

Barely able to see where his feet went, Mark set off down the highway. And he realized the evening wasn't so silent, after all. Night birds called out to each other, and his own sneakers padded over the asphalt in time with his heartbeat.

Something glided just over his head, its wings whispering softly. Mark couldn't make out the kind of bird, but thought it might be an owl. Stopping midstride, he watched as the creature suddenly dive-bombed the field. A high-pitched squeak followed. Apparently the owl had caught himself some dinner.

Mark was strolling along and feeling good, when a car's headlights beamed toward him in the distance. Squinting against the unwanted light, he stepped off the road, barely avoiding the drainage ditch. Moments later, the car whizzed past, a red sedan that looked like Stacy's. But she was miles away at the Dawsons'.

A few yards down the road, the brake lights lit. The car stopped, then backed toward him.

It *was* Stacy.

She rolled down her window and poked her head out. "Mark? I thought that was you."

"Hey," he said.

The light wind lifted locks of her hair, tempting him to reach out and tuck those wayward strands behind her ears. He desperately needed to back away, but the ditch prevented that.

"What are you doing out here?" Stacy asked. "Did your car stall or something?"

Mark shook his head. "Needed some air."

"But you're at least three miles from the clinic."

Was he? He had no idea how far he'd gone. "Aren't you supposed to be at the Dawsons'?" he asked.

"I was, but I just left."

"Did you enjoy yourself?"

"Very much, thanks. How was golf?"

"Great," he said. He'd enjoyed both the game and the two men who'd joined him and Will. "Did you visit Tom today?"

"Yes, and he looks good—you'll see for yourself tomorrow. By the way, they moved him to the cardio-rehab wing. He's pretty crabby about the exercises they make him do, and he hates his new low-fat, low-sodium diet." She waved her hand. "I'm sure you'll hear all about that."

"No doubt."

Silence.

Mark searched his mind for something else to say, but his muddied brain refused to cooperate.

"You probably don't want to walk all the way back to the clinic," Stacy said. "Do you need a ride?"

What he needed was a woman—*this* woman. No, what he *needed* was self-control. Mark shoved his hands in his pockets and shook his head. "I'd rather walk."

"It's a good night for that," Stacy said.

Her face was an open book. Even with the wine clouding his judgment, he saw the yearning there. He had no doubt that if he asked her to join him, she would.

He wanted very much to do just that, but given his feelings and the romance of this place, being alone with her out here was out of the question. Tonight, being anywhere near her was dangerous.

Mark rocked back on his heels. "See you."

"Oh," she said. "Right. Enjoy."

"Thanks. I will."

Standing in the road, he watched the taillights of her car until they disappeared.

As MARK LEFT THE CARDIO-REHAB wing of the hospital Sunday afternoon, he mentally swiped his brow. The visit hadn't been pleasant, but Stacy had warned him. Tom had been in a bad mood, grumpy and not wanting company. He hadn't even gloated over forcing Mark to stay in town. All in all, though, he looked good and was progressing nicely.

Before exiting the building, Mark wandered into the pharmacy on the ground floor. There, he found razor blades, which he'd forgotten to pick up at Spenser's. On his way to the fresh flowers in a bucket by the cash register, he passed a wall of hair products. The clips caught his eye. He selected a package of two slender, gold barrettes for Stacy.

In the next aisle, he grabbed a box of condoms. He couldn't have said why. Hoping to get lucky, he guessed. Since he only wanted one woman and didn't intend to act on his feelings, that was a joke.

Shortly after six o'clock, he pulled to a stop in front of Val and Silas's place, the flowers and a six-pack on the seat beside him. Several other cars were parked in the short driveway and on the strip out front. Apparently Mark wasn't the only one invited to dinner.

The Masons lived in a small, tidy house with a huge yard in a sparsely inhabited neighborhood similar to Stacy's. Which got Mark wondering how she'd spent her afternoon. He imagined her in her backyard, soaking up the sun in a skimpy bikini, her breasts almost spilling out, and those long legs…

With a frown, he cut off the fantasy. He didn't want to think about Stacy's breasts, her legs or any other part of her delectable body. He didn't want to think about her, period. Tonight was about relaxing and eating great barbecue.

The sounds of laughter told him the party was out back. Bypassing the house, Mark headed across the side yard and through an open gate.

On the patio, Silas's grill hissed and smoked, sending out a smell that made Mark's belly growl. At a nearby table, Val was arranging snack food, and hungry guests had gathered around. After stopping to greet Silas, Mark headed over to Val.

He handed her the flowers. "These are for you."

"Thank you, Dr. Mark. They're beautiful. I'm so glad you made it." She gestured at a man about Mark's age. "Have you and Cody met?"

Shaking his head, Mark extended his arm. "Mark Engle."

"Cody Naylor." The man had a firm grip and a level gaze.

Val pointed to a large ice chest beside the table. "Stick your six-pack in there, and help yourself to anything you find. I'll see you both later." She wandered off to greet other guests.

Standing around the chips and dip, Mark and Cody chatted.

"I spent ten years in Silicon Valley," Cody told him. "Now I live here."

"You moved from Silicon Valley to Saddlers Prairie." Incredulous, Mark gaped at him. "Why?"

"Some would say I grew up here," Cody said without explaining further. "This is a pretty decent place to live, but I came back because my dad—my foster dad—is sick."

"What's wrong with him?" Mark asked.

"Pancreatic cancer."

A painful and deadly cancer rarely diagnosed until it had progressed too far. Mark felt for Cody and his foster father.

"He tried a couple of experimental drugs that helped for a few years, but now..." Cody kicked at the grass. "There's nothing left to try. At the moment, he's stable, but...I went ahead and lined up a couple of round-the-clock nurses."

"Sorry to hear that," Mark said.

"Thanks, man."

Cody changed the subject. They talked about doing a day hike in the hills the following weekend, then something made Mark glance over his shoulder.

Stacy was entering the backyard.

As Stacy drove slowly past the Masons' house in search of a place to park, she squinted at one particular vehicle—Mark's.

Her jaw dropped.

It had been bad enough seeing him on the highway last night. If only she'd driven past. But no. Worried that he was stranded, she'd taken the trouble to stop.

As she maneuvered her car between two trucks, she recalled the way the bright moonlight had cast Mark's face in shadow so that she could barely make out his expression. His dark eyes had glittered with something potent yet indefinable, a look that had touched her in ways she didn't understand and couldn't seem to forget—even after he'd all but told her to leave him alone.

Determined to do just that and push him from her thoughts, she'd sternly reminded herself that longing for Mark would lead only to heartache.

Fat lot of good that did. Keyed up, she'd lain awake for a while before finally calming down enough to asleep.

This morning, she'd awakened feeling much better. She'd barely thought of Mark today, and even then only fleetingly. But now... Couldn't she have this one day without him in it?

Cradling the bottle of wine she'd brought, Stacy exited the car. From the number of vehicles and the raised voices coming from the backyard, it seemed Val and Silas had invited a big crowd. With so many people milling around, seeing Mark wouldn't be so bad.

At the open front door, she peered through the screen. "Hello?" she called.

No one replied. Apparently everyone was out back. Stacy headed around the side of the house, her strapless sundress inching down until it was uncomfortably low. She'd bought the dress online, mostly for the built-in cups that enabled her to go braless. She hadn't considered it might slip, but then her breasts *were* on the small size.

Fervently wishing she'd worn a dress with straps, she tugged up her top and pasted a friendly smile on her face. There. Now she was ready to face Mark.

All the same, she faltered inside the open gate that abutted the backyard. Her unwitting gaze sought him out. Tall and handsome in a navy golf shirt and reflector sunglasses, he was easy to find. He looked relaxed, gesturing with a can of beer and chatting with Cody Naylor on the far side of the yard. As if he felt her stare, he glanced her way.

Thanks to the sunglasses and the distance between them, Stacy couldn't see his eyes or read his expression. All the same, she felt the heat in his gaze. Heat she neither wanted nor needed, especially here in public. Swallowing, she tore her attention from him.

And noted Val moving toward her. Judging by the shrewd quirk of her lips, the older woman had caught Stacy ogling Mark. Stacy blushed and at the same time cringed. As friendly as Val was, she was also notorious for broadcasting what she called "breaking news."

Not about to give the woman fodder for her gossip mill,

Stacy made up her mind to all but ignore Mark. Smiling, she said, "Hello, Val. How's your elbow today?"

"Thanks to Dr. Mark, much, much better." Val shot her an appraising glance. "You look lovely today."

"Thanks." Stacy held on to her smile. "Mark *is* a great doctor."

"With looks and brains and a good 'bedside manner.' That man is a real catch." Val winked, then lowered her voice. "I hope you two get a chance to socialize this afternoon."

This was too much. Eager to get away from her, Stacy handed over the wine bottle. "This is for you. Those ribs smell wonderful. I think I'll say hello to Silas." Then she'd warn Mark about Val.

She greeted Silas and stopped to chat with other guests before making her way toward Mark and Cody.

"Hello, Cody." She smiled. "How's Phil?"

"Holding his own—for now." Cody's gaze traveled over her. "I like that dress."

"Thank you." She tugged up the top.

Cody was handsome and rich, but didn't seem to care about money. He'd even sold his lucrative business and moved back to Saddlers Prairie to spend time with his foster father before he died. Cody was a man with values Stacy shared, but except as a friend, she wasn't attracted to him. He felt the same way about her.

She turned to Mark, whose silvery sunglasses were trained on her. "Hi," she said. "Could I talk to you a moment—privately?"

"Sure. Do you mind, Cody?"

Cody glanced from Stacy to Mark, then arched his eyebrows. "Nope. I need another beer. I'll see you two around."

He sauntered off.

"You look great," Mark said. "I didn't expect to see you here."

"I didn't even know about the barbecue until I got home last night. Val left a voice message on my landline, inviting me. She never said a word about asking you."

"Isn't that a coincidence—she invited me when I ran into her at Spenser's late yesterday afternoon," Mark said.

"That's what I wanted to tell you," Stacy warned. "She's trying to fix us up."

They both glanced at Val, who was chatting with several female friends, all of them blatantly watching her and Mark. Wearing matching smiles and knowing looks, the women waved.

"Not exactly subtle, is she?" Mark snorted. "As I said before, one of the things I detest about small towns is the way people stick their noses into everyone else's business."

This time, Stacy had to agree.

"If they think we're getting together," he muttered, "they're crazy. I'll only be here two more weeks. Don't they *get* that?"

"Apparently not."

"Let's not fan any fires. For the rest of the barbecue, we stay away from each other."

Stacy nodded. "Agreed."

They turned in opposite directions.

For the next hour, Stacy didn't so much as glance in Mark's direction—not openly, anyway. All the same, she was keenly aware of his presence. A fine tension hummed inside her, starting low in her stomach and fanning through her entire body.

Once or twice she felt his eyes on her, yet when she checked he was always looking someplace else. She just hoped Val noticed how little they socialized.

By the time Silas grilled the last of the ribs, the sun was slanting toward the horizon. Her mouth watering, Stacy loaded her paper plate with food, then searched out a seat at one of the two joined picnic tables.

By tacit agreement, she and Mark sat at opposite ends. She chatted and laughed with the people around her, and out of the corner of her eye, noticed Mark doing the same thing.

By the time the sun set and Val and Silas lit the tiki lights, Stacy wished she'd brought a shawl to keep her warm. Cold and ready to leave, she sought out Val, who was in the kitchen with several other women. "Would you like help cleaning up?" Stacy offered.

"No, honey. You go enjoy yourself."

"Actually, I need to get home, but thanks for inviting me. The food was delicious."

What about Mark? Val's curious glance seemed to say, but Stacy managed an innocent look and the woman didn't ask. "Come back anytime, Stacy."

As she pushed through the screen door, she saw Mark striding toward his car.

They were leaving at the same time. Stacy didn't want to know what Val and her friends would think about that.

"Bye, Mark," she called out, for Val's benefit. "See you tomorrow."

"Night."

Stacy started the car and turned on her headlights. Mark followed her out of the neighborhood and onto the highway, staying behind her as he had the night he'd followed her home then driven them both to Barb's.

Several miles from Val and Silas's, in the middle of no-where, he honked his horn, then honked twice more.

Frowning, Stacy glanced in the rearview mirror. What did he want? Whatever it was, it must be important. She signaled, then followed a dirt path that led behind a small grove of trees just off the highway. There she braked to a stop.

Mark pulled up behind her.

"What's the problem?" she asked, sticking her head out the window.

He slid out of his sedan and shut the door. "Get out of the car."

"What for? Did Val say something to upset you?"

"This isn't about Val. Just do it."

"Yes, sir, Mr. Drill Sergeant," Stacy muttered as she complied.

She was barely on her feet when Mark approached her. Without a word, he pulled her close and kissed her.

Chapter Eleven

Caught by surprise, Stacy stiffened. But Mark held her tightly, his lips teasing and coaxing, sending delicious warmth through her. She melted against him.

"You're cold," he said, running his hands up her bare arms and shoulders.

"Not anymore." She pulled his head back down for another kiss.

Groaning, he urged her lips apart and devoured her mouth. Kisses that were deep, demanding, urgent—everything she'd dreamed of since that night at her front door.

She didn't care about people talking, or whether this was wrong or that she was bound to get hurt someday. All that mattered was right here, right now.

Still kissing her, his body pressed tightly to hers, Mark walked her backward until she bumped against something. The fender of his car. He lifted her onto the hood, then joined her there.

The metal was warm and unyielding against her bottom, and when he gently pushed her back, the windshield felt cold and hard. As soon as he kissed her again, she forgot about any discomfort.

Under a blanket of stars and the brilliant moon, lost in a haze of desire, she exchanged wet, wild kisses with Mark, while they groped each other like high school kids.

He slid his hand down the top of her dress, then hesitated. "You're not wearing a bra."

"This kind of dress doesn't need one."

"I didn't realize..." He swallowed hard. "You don't know what that does to me."

Seconds ticked by. Eternity. Would he never do what she so desperately ached for? Stacy moaned. "Please, Mark, touch me." She started to pull her top down.

Mark stopped her. "Let me." With hands that trembled, he tugged her dress below her breasts.

The soft fabric and cool night air teased her sensitive nipples, making them stand out.

For a few moments, he simply stared. In the soft moonlight, Stacy saw the raw hunger in his eyes—hunger for her.

"You're beautiful," he murmured.

She was smaller than she wanted to be, but wasn't about to argue. If he—

His fingers feathered lightly over her puckered nipples, and she lost her train of thought.

Her senses alive, she closed her eyes. His breath blew warm on her breast. His hair tickled her skin. His velvet lips closed sensuously around her sensitive nipple. Pulling gently, he swirled the nub with his tongue...

Someone whimpered. Her own self, she realized. Clutching the back of Mark's head, she urged him closer. Dampness flooded her panties. He moved to the other breast, repeating the pleasure. The soft night breeze was almost painful on the wet, swollen peak.

Craving his attention down lower, she shifted restlessly against the hood of the car. Bright lights flashed in her head.

Mark stilled, swore and jerked her dress back over her breasts.

Stacy opened her eyes and saw Sheriff Gabe Bennett, flashlight in hand, striding toward her and Mark.

"Stay here," Mark warned in a low voice. He slid off the hood.

MARK SQUINTED AND HELD UP his hands, shielding his eyes from the bright light of the flashlight.

"It's you two." Amusement danced across Gabe Bennett's face. "I figured you for a couple of teenagers using Daddy's car. You're parked in a popular hangout."

Mark hadn't known that. He'd honked at Stacy because after hours of torture, he wanted her too badly to think straight.

What was it about her that turned his self-control on its head?

Instead of waiting at the car, she'd followed him toward Bennett. Lips slightly swollen and hair every which way, she looked as if she'd been thoroughly kissed. Her arms wrapped around her waist, she chewed her lower lip, and Mark knew she was embarrassed and a little worried.

Feeling fiercely protective, he stepped in front of her. "Can't two people look at the stars?" he asked.

The sheriff snickered. "That's a good one. We all know you and Stacy weren't looking at anything but each other, though I doubt either of you had your eyes open."

"You won't tell anyone about this, will you?" Stacy asked, clearly anxious.

"You think the attraction between you two is some big secret?" Bennett chuckled. "It's all over town that after you left that dinner at the mayor's last week, you stood on Stacy's doorstep for an unusually long time. You weren't stargazing then, either."

Stacy buried her face in her hands and groaned. "How do you know about that?"

"The night has a thousand eyes."

Mark wanted to punch out every one of them. "You didn't say anything at golf yesterday."

"Neither did you, and I figured it was your call."

"Please don't tell anyone, Gabe," Stacy said. "Please."

"It's not my business to go around gossiping. But do me a favor—next time the mating urge grabs you two, take it to the privacy of one of your homes."

As Gabe pulled his vehicle onto the highway, Mark swore. Of all the half-witted, stupid... He'd never acted so impulsively. Bothered and astonished by his own behavior, he gave a derisive snort. "I totally lost my head tonight."

"We both did." Stacy blew the hair out of her eyes. "What is this crazy pull between us?"

"It's called chemistry, and we seem to have more than our share of it."

"It scares me."

Mark, too. He'd never felt so obsessed with a woman that he forgot where he was, forgot to even think. He prized himself on his discipline and control and his ability to behave rationally in any emergency, traits that had carried him through med school and made him a good doctor. He never lost his cool, never let down his guard. Never.

Until he'd met Stacy.

His plan for the future didn't include getting involved with a beautiful woman in Saddlers Prairie. But tonight he'd forgotten that plan, had kissed and touched her until they were both hot and needy.

He was in a dangerous place. Yet he wanted more.

What in hell was happening to him?

Not at all sure what to do, he walked Stacy to her car, both of them as quiet as the night. He opened her door, and without a word, she slid into her seat.

Her damned hair was in her face again. Mark wished

he had those barrettes, but he'd left them at the apartment. Reaching through the window, he smoothed the flyaway hair behind her ears.

She barely reacted. She looked a little dazed. Mark was right there with her. Truth was, he felt as if he'd been struck by lightning.

Straightening, he glanced at the star-studded sky and waited for Stacy to start the engine. She just sat there, staring into space.

"Hey." Unable to keep his hands to himself, he leaned in again and touched her cheek. "You okay?"

"I don't know." She looked up at him, her eyes big and somber. "I think so. I just hope Gabe keeps his word. If Val and the others find out about tonight, we'll never hear the end of it."

"Gabe's a decent man. He promised to keep quiet, and he will," Mark assured her. If not… Mark had never been a violent man, but if Bennett reneged, if he hurt Stacy in any way, he just might become one.

He drove back to the clinic, already anticipating the next time he kissed her.

QUESTIONS SWIRLED THROUGH Stacy's mind as she headed for work Monday morning. Would Mark apologize? Should she? Was there anything to apologize *for,* and now what?

The same questions had kept her awake and haunted her sleep last night, which did nothing for her nerves. Stomach churning, she let herself into the clinic.

She barely blinked before the man who'd starred in her dreams loped down the stairs. His hair was still damp, and the subtle scent of pine soap tickled pleasantly in her nostrils. Wearing a pressed blue oxford shirt, dark pants and loafers, he looked his usual incredibly handsome self. Feelings she didn't want to acknowledge engulfed her—desire, tenderness and awkwardness.

"Good morning." Avoiding his gaze, she toyed with the ends of her shawl.

Mark had seen her bare breasts, had taken her nipples into his mouth and heard her moan with pleasure last night, so why she felt shy this morning was anyone's guess.

"Hi. You're bright and colorful today."

His gaze traveled over her magenta flared skirt and peach peasant blouse, his intent expression reminding her of the instant before he'd pulled her close and kissed her last night. The fine hum in her body that was always with her lately kicked in to high gear, along with a flood of familiar heat.

And here it was not quite seven-thirty in the morning, with a packed day ahead.

Forcing herself to turn away from his magnetic, smoldering eyes, Stacy hung up the shawl. "The weather people are predicting rain today," she said, just to break the charged silence.

"The farmers will be grateful."

Stacy stowed her purse and knitting in the desk drawer.

"I believe you're on coffee duty this week," he said.

Apparently he wasn't going to bring up last night. Well, neither would she, no matter how badly she wanted to. Mark might think she was needy or, even worse, a nag, as Vince had whenever she'd questioned him about their future.

"I'll start a pot right away," she said brightly.

She spun toward the hall, Mark falling into step beside her. Suddenly she yawned so hard, her eyes watered.

He gave her a sideways glance. "That was some big yawn. Did you stay up late?"

Not about to admit to her lack of sleep, Stacy simply said, "I could've used an extra hour this morning."

"I was pretty keyed up, too. Last night was crazy."

Not sure exactly what he meant, she busied herself with the coffeemaker and waited for him to say more. But he was silent.

Maybe he was as confused about what was happening between them as she was. Except, she wasn't confused. The truth was, she understood her own feelings perfectly. She not only desired Mark, she also *really* liked him. As risky as that was to her well-being, she no longer cared.

"I don't usually act like that," Mark finally said.

Was that an apology? Stacy raised her eyebrows, and so did he.

"Are we okay?" he asked.

She forced a bright smile. "You tell me."

"I'm good if you are." She nodded, and apparently satisfied, he blew out an audible breath. "Hey, I got you something at the hospital gift shop yesterday."

If he wanted to change the subject, fine. "You did?" Stacy couldn't imagine what it was.

"Here." He pulled a small bag from his hip pocket and handed it to her.

Curious, she peered inside and pulled the gift out... A pair of gold barrettes? "These are very pretty, Mark. Thanks."

"They'll keep your hair out of your eyes."

"How thoughtful. I'll try them on now. Just give me a minute."

Stacy closeted herself in the bathroom and attached the barrettes so that they anchored her hair in place. She liked the effect, which made her look— *Wait a minute*.

Narrowing her eyes at her reflection, she leaned closer to the mirror. Was that a love bite near her collarbone? It definitely was. Somehow she hadn't noticed this morning. She needed her concealer, and now.

Forgetting about the barrettes, she exited the bathroom to grab her purse.

"I like your hair that way," Mark said.

"Me, too. Why didn't you tell me about the mark on my neck?"

"I figured you knew it was there."

"If I did, I'd have worn a turtleneck. Do you think I *want* people wondering about my love life? Excuse me while I fix the problem."

A moment later, having liberally applied concealer over the redness, she returned to the kitchen. "Do you see anything now?"

Mark moved in close to check. "Nothing but your beautiful neck." He ran his finger from behind her ear to the sensitive crook of her shoulder. "You are so damn sexy."

Her knees actually threatened to buckle.

Tipping her chin up, he kissed her, a slow, delicious kiss that spread bone-melting heat through her. She leaned into him, her eyes drifting closed. He was aroused, which just made her want him more.

Suddenly he released her and swore. "I had no intention of going near you this morning," he said. "But for some reason when we're together, I can't keep my hands off you."

Brain in a fog, she blinked slowly. He was watching her with his dark, hooded eyes, only increasing her desire.

"I tell myself to stay away, but then I catch a whiff of your perfume, or you look at me with those big eyes and purse your lips the slightest bit, and I *have* to touch you. Your mouth turns me on." His thumb caressed her bottom lip, and she shivered. "I love how you respond to me."

The electricity between them was so powerful, she couldn't fight it, either. Somehow she managed to pull herself together and step out of his reach. "What are we doing, Mark?"

"Passing a few extremely pleasant minutes while the coffee brews." A sputtering issued from the coffeemaker, and he smiled. "And it's ready."

With those words, Stacy finally understood. She was a distraction for Mark, someone to keep him occupied until he left town.

What an idiot she was, thinking he might have feelings for her when she knew he was leaving town in less than two weeks.

Thank God she'd wised up before things went any further and she made an even bigger fool of herself.

Oblivious of her thoughts, Mark whistled softly and filled two mugs. "Here you go," he said.

Stacy accepted hers without meeting his gaze.

"Something wrong?" he asked, sounding puzzled.

Very observant, Doctor. Offering a poor attempt at a smile, she added milk and sugar to her mug. "Why would you think that?"

"Because you're frowning and you won't look at me. What'd I do?"

Her spoon clinked loudly against her mug. "You're a smart man. Figure it out."

"I honestly don't know. At least give me a hint."

What was the point of discussing the matter? Mark had his future all mapped out, and she wasn't in it. "I'd rather not."

He scratched the back of his neck. "Come on, Stace, I have no—"

The phone rang, and she pivoted toward the hall. "I need to get that."

Mark caught hold of her hand. "Just this once, let the answering service pick up."

Wanting only to get away from him, she twisted out of his grasp. "It's my job to answer the phone."

He gave a curt nod. "Fine. Go. But this conversation isn't over."

Chapter Twelve

Dumbfounded, Mark stared after Stacy. One minute she was in his arms, kissing him with an eagerness that matched his own and fueling his hunger. The next, she was giving him a dirty look that made him feel about two inches tall.

Bad enough that he couldn't seem to control himself around her. Now she was mad at him, too?

Clueless as to what had caused the sudden change, he took his coffee into the office and shut the door. Standing at the window, he stared broodingly through the slats in the blind, barely noticing the rolling prairies.

Things between him and Stacy had seemed fine this morning—until those amazing kisses. He thought back, running through the conversation for hints of any issues, and came up blank.

You're a smart man. Figure it out.

Mark snorted. He was smart about some things, but not women.

The intercom buzzed. Leaning forward, he answered warily. "Yeah?"

"It's Dr. Willis from the imaging center, calling about Anita," Stacy said.

Mark grabbed a pen and paper. "Put her through."

Minutes later, he hung up, opened his door and headed for the waiting room.

Stacy was at her desk, tapping a pencil to her lips as she studied the daily schedule she'd printed. Her brow was slightly furrowed and she looked cute.

One glance at him, and she dropped the pencil and sat up straight. "And?"

Mark smiled. "The biopsy was normal and the mammogram identified a benign cyst. Dr. Willis found no indication of cancer, but Anita will need to have the cyst surgically excised."

"That's wonderful news!" Stacy's laughter bubbled out, so light and sweet that Mark chuckled, too. "Anita will be so relieved," she went on. "She told everyone that she had cancer. I guess now she'll have to un-tell them."

Her smile lingered, and for one long moment Mark thought that all was well between them.

Wrong.

Abruptly, the joyful expression faded and the corners of her mouth turned down. Stymied, he shifted his weight. He wanted to clear the air, but with Anita to phone and the clinic due to open shortly, now was not the time.

"Would you pull Anita's—" he began, but Stacy was already handing him the file and today's schedule. "Thanks— and we *will* talk later."

She managed a brief nod.

Mark returned to the office and made the call.

Relieved at her prognosis, Anita chattered brightly. At least *someone* was happy this morning. His thoughts on Stacy, Mark barely heard anything the woman said. If Stacy kept up the aloof act, it was going to be a long day. He'd just have to—

"Dr. Mark?" Anita asked. "Are you still there?"

"I should go," he said. "My first appointment will be here any second."

Forty minutes later, he taped the gauze bandage he'd carefully wrapped around Harlan Kittredge's thumb. Over the weekend, the rancher had slammed the barn door on it and had shown up unscheduled and in excruciating pain. After administering a tetanus shot, Mark had drained the excess fluid from under the nail, and the pain had all but faded.

"You'll want to keep the nail clean for at least ten days," he told the rancher.

"I got a manger to muck out," Kittredge said. "Two hundred cows have given birth there since March. What with the rains we had in April and all that manure, the place is a stinky mess."

Mark could just imagine. "You don't want an infection," he said, handing over several pairs of latex gloves. "Wear these under your work gloves and wash your hands thoroughly and often, and you should be all right."

Kittredge gave the gloves a wary look, but shoved them into his jeans pocket. He was leaving the office when Anita waltzed past him, looking as if she'd won the lottery.

Short skirt flouncing, she strutted right up to Mark, wrapped her arms around him and held on tight.

Not sure what to do, he stood still with his hands outstretched. "Uh, hello," he said. "I didn't expect to see you this morning."

She frowned slightly and gazed up at him. "I told you I was coming in."

Mark didn't recall that, but then he'd been preoccupied.

Standing in the open office door, Kittredge and the other patients in the waiting room watched with interest.

"Don't strangle the man," someone quipped.

Anita finally let go. "I can't help myself," she said, sniffling. "I've never been so relieved in my life." She studied Mark's hair with a critical eye. "When you're ready for a trim, come see me. Anytime, no appointment needed. I'll make room for you, no matter what."

She turned her attention to two matronly women. "In case

you didn't hear the good news, I found out this morning that I don't have breast cancer! It's a benign cyst."

Everyone cheered, and Anita dipped her head as if she were on stage, acknowledging applause.

Arms crossed, Mark sat on the corner of his desk and watched the performance. He caught sight of Stacy, standing behind everyone else. She gave him a this-is-so-Anita look, and he nodded in silent agreement. For that moment, all was right with the world.

"Don't forget to get your mammogram, ladies," Anita said. "And, Bert and Jake, remind your wives to get theirs. From now on, I'll be getting one every year, just to make sure I'm okay." She glanced at her watch. "My customers are waiting for their haircuts, and I'd better scoot. I can't wait to share my good news with them!"

When the front door shut behind her, everyone was smiling, Mark included. He beckoned the next patient into his office.

STACY WAS TIDYING UP FROM the morning rush and getting ready to eat a quick lunch before the afternoon onslaught when Sarah Jane and Byron trudged through the door. One look at the couple, and she knew something was wrong. As before, they were holding hands, but both looked pale and seemed in low spirits.

"We need to see Dr. Mark," Byron said. He sounded as if he had swollen glands.

Mark was still in the office, probably playing catch-up.

Wanting to give him a heads-up, she asked, "Can I tell him why you're here?"

Sarah Jane nodded dully. "We're both sick with bad sore throats." Her voice was soft, as if talking hurt.

"And we're really tired," Byron added.

What they described could be strep or mono or any number of things, Stacy thought as she stood. "I'll let Dr. Mark know. Have a seat."

She knocked on the office door, then slipped inside. "Byron and Sarah Jane are back."

Seated at the desk, Mark glanced up. "So they've decided Sarah Jane should get on birth control. When two people are that hot for each other, holding back is difficult."

Didn't they both know it.

Avoiding his intent gaze, Stacy glanced down. "I don't know that sex is on their minds right now. They're both sick."

He nodded. "Pull their files and send them back."

Ten minutes later, the couple returned to the waiting area, followed by Mark, who probably wanted to head upstairs and eat before this afternoon's scheduled appointments started.

"Dr. Mark is sending our blood samples out to be tested, but he's pretty sure we have mono," Sarah Jane told Stacy. She gave Byron a dirty look. "There's only one girl in the school you could've caught it from, and that's Cindy Jones. You kissed her because I decided I'm not ready to have sex with you, didn't you?" Her expression darkened. "Maybe you two did more than kiss."

What little color remained in her boyfriend's cheeks drained away. "I didn't kiss her, I swear."

Sarah Jane didn't seem to have heard. "She's always been interested in you, Byron, and you know it. I guess you're interested in her, too."

"No, I'm not!"

Couples didn't usually air their dirty laundry in the doctor's office, but these teenagers didn't seem to care. Stacy glanced at Mark, who seemed every bit as intrigued by Sarah Jane's outburst as Stacy.

"It's true that mono is known as the kissing disease and is spread through contact with saliva," he said calmly. "But kissing isn't the only way to contract the disease."

"Well, I can't think of any other way a person has contact with saliva," Sarah Jane replied, glaring at Byron.

"Actually, there are many other ways," Mark said. "Eating from the same plate or drinking from the same straw are common ways to spread the disease."

Byron looked as if a lightbulb had gone on in his mind. "That's it!" he said. "Before Cindy got mono, we ran into each other at the Burger Palace, and she let me taste her strawberry-marshmallow milkshake to show me it wasn't as gross as it sounded." He frowned. "Only thing is, she wasn't sick then."

"Sometimes the symptoms don't show up for weeks, but the carrier is still contagious," Mark explained.

"That has to be it." Byron gave Sarah Jane a pleading look. "I don't want anyone but you, Sarah Jane—I haven't since the first time I kissed you last September."

Stacy almost melted at the romantic declaration, but Sarah Jane snorted and crossed her skinny arms. "I want to go home now and lie down."

"You both should do that," Mark said. "I'll call your parents and let them know about the blood tests. Meantime, I want you both to go to bed and rest, drink plenty of liquids and stay home from school for a week to ten days, until you feel better and I give the okay. I'll call and check on you later in the week, and I want to see you back here in ten days."

"We'll schedule that follow-up appointment now," Stacy said.

Sarah Jane nodded, and without a glance at poor Byron, she set up an appointment. Byron scheduled his at the same time.

The girl marched out of the office. Looking more miserable than he had when he'd first come in, Byron followed her without a goodbye to Stacy or Mark.

"I feel for them," Stacy said. "But they certainly are dramatic."

"All teenagers are. They're good kids, though. I like them both."

So did Stacy. "Do you think Byron kissed another girl?" she asked.

"I doubt it. He's clearly in love with Sarah Jane."

"I think so, too, and I'm going to cross my fingers for them."

For a few long moments, Mark looked as if he wanted to say something. Then he glanced at his watch. "I need to eat before the afternoon appointments. We'll talk at the end of the day."

He waited for her nod, then headed up the stairs.

As the afternoon dwindled away, Stacy glanced at the wall clock with mounting dread. Mark expected a conversation about this morning, and she wasn't sure what to say.

While he was finishing up with the last appointment she washed the coffeepot and wiped down the kitchen counter. Then she straightened the office.

By the time the patient exited the clinic, Stacy was an anxious mess. With clammy hands, she pulled the drapes and hung the closed sign in the window. When she turned around, Mark was entering the room.

He gestured at a chair. "Please, sit down."

Somehow, having the desk between them seemed safer, and Stacy returned to her chair.

Instead of sitting, Mark leaned against the wall and eyed her. Not about to speak first, Stacy folded her hands and waited.

After a moment, he broke the silence. "Obviously you're mad at me, and I don't know what I did."

Stacy brushed imaginary debris from the desktop. "I'm

not mad, Mark." Only a silly fool, for hoping the attraction between them might turn into something meaningful.

"Then why won't you look at me?"

"Is this better?" Keeping her eyes wide and innocent, she met his gaze.

Mark snorted. "You've been freezing me out since this morning, and I deserve to know why."

Under his direct stare, she couldn't lie. "You're leaving soon."

"Yeah." He shrugged as if to say, *This is news?*

"What we were doing... If we keep on doing it... I refuse to be your temporary distraction."

There. She'd said it.

"Temporary..." Seeming utterly confused, Mark frowned. "Look, I like you."

"And I like *you*."

"Then what's the problem?"

Sometimes men were so dense. "Why did you honk for me to stop the car last night?"

"You strolled into the Masons' backyard in that little yellow dress." His lips curled into a semblance of a smile, as if he were remembering. "Those long legs, your bare shoulders, the way the dress hugged your hips and breasts—no normal, red-blooded guy could resist you. Not me, anyway. I wanted you." His dark eyes glinted with desire. "I still do."

If only he wouldn't look at her like that, as if he were starving to death and she was the food that would save him. Every nerve in her body strained toward him, *wanting* to feed him, and she was glad for the desk between them.

"You want me, too," he said, his gaze probing her very soul.

He knew her too well. Helpless, she nodded.

"Why shouldn't we enjoy ourselves?" Without taking his

gaze from her, he pushed away from the wall and started forward.

She'd never felt such intense physical desire in her life, the fire constantly simmering inside her, flaring up whenever Mark looked at her. Longing held her immobile.

Regardless, she wasn't about to give in, no matter how strong the need. Making love with Mark was far too risky.

As he started around the desk, she held up her hands, warning him to stop. "No more kisses, Mark."

Wearing a resigned expression, he nodded and stepped back.

"I'm going to leave now." With remarkably steady legs, she stood, hugging her purse to her chest as if the leather could shield her from his charms. "I'll see you tomorrow."

Feeling his gaze as keenly as if he were standing in front of her, she walked out.

TEMPORARY DISTRACTION. The words irritated Mark, and he clomped upstairs. Did she really believe he was using her as a distraction? She must think he was a total jerk.

That felt lousy, and his already low mood dipped further south. There was only one cure for clearing his head—a good run, something he'd neglected since arriving in town.

He changed into running clothes. In short time, he was squinting against the still-bright sun as he jogged up the road toward the highway. There he upped his speed and ran full-out, until sweat dripped off his body and stung his eyes and he was gasping for air. Leg muscles straining, he turned around and ran hard all the way back.

The run had done its job—he was exhausted, but felt great. After gulping several glasses of water, he stretched and cooled down, then enjoyed a tepid shower. Famished, he wolfed down half the rotisserie chicken he'd bought at Spenser's over the weekend.

His mind didn't kick into gear again until he pushed back from the table with the perfect solution to his problem.

He would simply stop wanting Stacy. Resisting temptation was nothing new. Years ago he'd turned down an offer of full-time work and the promise of someday managing Willett's General Store in Steer Bluff, and instead had put himself into debt by heading off to college. He'd studied when the rest of his friends were out partying and getting laid. Knowing he was taking the steps needed to fulfill his life plan had made the sacrifices easier.

Mark squared his shoulders. He was strong and disciplined, a man in control of himself and his life. He could resist his desires.

Starting right now, he no longer wanted Stacy.

Restless and frustrated despite the draining run, he paced the apartment and listed the reasons he no longer wanted her. The great job waiting for him and the beautiful women he was sure to meet. His generous salary and how that would help fulfil his life plan. Even the fact that Stacy thought he was using her as a distraction.

"I don't want her broken heart on my conscience," he reminded himself out loud.

He drummed the reasons into his head. Then his wayward mind countered with its own list.

Stacy was smart, organized and efficient, easy to talk to, and not afraid to share her opinion. Which made her infinitely enjoyable to be with. She was also beautiful and passionate, with smooth skin, silky hair, soft, welcoming lips and an amazing body....

His own body hardened. He swore.

She was in his blood, and there wasn't a damn thing he could do about it—except stay away from her.

Stacy would never know the depth of his hunger for her,

Chapter Thirteen

After a busy Monday and Tuesday, Wednesday morning was slow and leisurely, and the rest of the day looked no different. Even the phone was quiet. By early afternoon, Stacy had caught up on office work, enjoyed a long lunch, read three chapters of next month's book-club selection and finished several rows of the blanket she was nearly finished knitting for Megan's baby. Just in time for the shower on Saturday.

By two o'clock, she was all but twiddling her thumbs, and praying for a walk-in. Mark was in the office with the door closed, making calls, catching up on patient notes and avoiding her.

Stacy knew this because she was avoiding him, too. She hated the stiffness and formality that had sprung up between them, hated pretending that everything was fine when she was miserable.

Mark wasn't exactly Mr. Happy, either. Oh, he seemed friendly enough, but he wasn't the same as before. No more heated looks, and any conversation was brief and centered on patients.

She so wished Wayne at the temp agency would call with a replacement. If he wanted that bonus, he'd best find someone soon.

The intercom buzzed. With business this slow, Mark could

easily have come out and talked to her face-to-face. Stacy answered with a crisp "Yes?"

"Is Megan Dawson still our only appointment this afternoon?" he asked.

"That's right. She'll be here at three, for her thirty-six-week checkup."

"In that case, I'm making an executive decision. As soon as she leaves, we're closing up and taking the rest of the afternoon off."

Stacy hadn't shopped yet for party favors or food for Megan's shower and needed the extra time. She readily agreed. "I'll let the answering service know, and print out a note we can tack to the door with your pager number."

After taking care of those tasks, she pulled out the baby blanket and knitting needles.

A good thirty minutes before Megan was due for her appointment, Opal Farraday, an octogenarian widow who still lived on her own, toddled in, toting her enormous handbag and a brown paper bag. Mark had seen her the previous day for a checkup.

Stacy stuffed the knitting into a drawer and jumped up to help the woman with her things. "Hello, Mrs. Farraday. What are you doing back here?"

"I baked a pie for Dr. Mark. Is he free?"

Poor and fiercely proud, the woman always paid her medical bill with baked goods, a practice that had been okayed by Dr. Tom.

"He'll love that," Stacy said, knowing Mark would prefer money. But if the clinic insisted on that, Mrs. Farraday wouldn't come back. "Please sit down while I get him."

Rather than use the intercom, Stacy knocked on Mark's door. "May I come in?"

"Sure."

Glancing from the file on the desk, Mark raised his eyebrows in question.

She shut the door. "Opal Farraday is here," she said.

"I saw her yesterday, and she seemed fine. Is she ill?"

Stacy shook her head. "She brought in her payment."

"Just deposit it with the other money." He scribbled a note on someone's file.

"You don't understand, Mark. She doesn't pay with money. She baked you a pie and would like to give it to you herself."

He rolled his eyes, which was about the reaction Stacy had expected.

"Hey, I've tasted her pies, and they're wonderful," she said. "Dr. Tom always comes out and thanks her—it's what she's used to."

Muttering, Mark set down the pen. In the waiting room, he greeted Opal Farraday with a pleasant enough expression. "Hello again, Mrs. Farraday."

"Hello, Dr. Mark." The old woman pushed heavily to her feet, then gestured at the bag on the chair beside her. "I baked you one of my deep-dish apple pies."

"My grandma used to make those." Mark peeked into the bag, sniffing appreciatively. "This looks delicious. Thank you."

"My pleasure." Her weathered cheeks rounded in a smile. "Back in nineteen seventy-five, this pie won a blue ribbon at the Montana State Fair. Since then, I've improved on the recipe. Not to brag, but you're in for a real treat. Isn't he, Stacy?"

Stacy hadn't eaten much at lunch, and the aroma of apples and cinnamon made her mouth water. "He certainly is."

She wrote out *Paid in Full* on the bill, and handed Mrs. Farraday a copy.

"Best have at it now, while it's still warm from the oven," the woman said.

"I'll do that," Mark said, with an eager expression that stripped years from his face.

Stacy pictured him as an excited little boy. How often had his family indulged him with a treat? His grandmother had died when he was young. Had his mother ever baked him a pie?

Mrs. Farraday beamed. "Be sure to share some with Stacy. She looks a bit peaked."

"I do?" Stacy frowned. "I feel just fine."

Mark studied her, not as a woman he desired, but as a patient.

Missing his intensity and warmth, she offered her arm to Mrs. Farraday. "Let me walk you to your car."

STACY WAS TAKING A LONG time to return to the clinic. Mark peered through the window and understood why. Opal Farraday moved about as fast as a turtle with no place to go. She probably shouldn't be driving. He'd ask Stacy to pull her file, then contact the woman's son about that.

The aroma of fresh-baked apple pie filled his nostrils. His stomach growled. Megan Dawson wasn't due for another twenty minutes, giving him ample time to enjoy a piece now.

Mrs. Farraday had been right about Stacy. She looked pale, but with things between them so tense, Mark didn't feel great, either.

Even if they were keeping a careful distance from each other, they could still share this pie. In search of a knife, two plates and two forks, he headed for the kitchen.

"I DON'T THINK MRS. FARRADAY should be driving anymore," Stacy said when she returned to the clinic. "I also think she needs new glasses, because I am not 'peaked.'"

Mark didn't comment. He was seated in a waiting-room

chair with a plate containing a generous wedge of pie on his knees.

"That looks so good," she said.

"You're telling me." He licked his lips, then grinned. "I cut you a slice and put it on your desk."

He hadn't smiled in days. Grateful that Mrs. Farraday's gift seemed to have eased the tension between them, Stacy smiled in return.

"Oh, yum," she said, rubbing her hands together as she sat down. "You were very nice to her."

He stared hard at Stacy. "I'm not some heartless bastard. You forget, I grew up poor."

For a minute there, Stacy *had* forgotten. "Did your mom pay the doctor bills with food?"

Mark shook his head. "She never was much of a cook. We didn't see doctors except for emergencies, but when we did, she paid in dribs and drabs."

Even Stacy's less-than-comfortable childhood had included regular checkups. "You said your grandma baked, though."

"She was a great cook. When we lived with her, she let me help." Pie apparently forgotten, Mark stared into space as if lost in memories.

"You lived with her?"

He nodded. "Mom needed someone to watch us while she worked, and Grandma had two spare rooms. She liked the company."

Stacy took advantage of his willingness to open up about his past. "If you don't mind my asking, how did she die?"

"Ovarian cancer. She was the one who first put the idea of being a doctor in my head. She thought I was smart and said that maybe someday I'd become a doctor and help sick people like her. For years, I never dared to dream I'd go into medicine, but those words stayed with me."

Stacy shook her head. "How old was she when she died?"

"Forty-seven."

"That's so young. You must've been little."

"I was nine, and Kevin was seven."

"Her death must've been difficult for you."

"You don't know the half of it. Grandma had been paying the rent, which we couldn't afford. We'd barely buried her when we had to move. Mom didn't have money for an apartment, so we lived in the car for months until she somehow saved enough."

No wonder Mark hadn't allowed himself to dream of being a doctor. Hurting for the boy he'd been and for his family, Stacy touched her hand to her heart. "Where was your dad?"

Mark snorted. "Where he always was—on the road, giving away his paycheck. I wonder how this pie will compare with my grandma's." He bent over his plate, letting Stacy know the conversation was over. "Cheers," he said, saluting her with his fork.

Stacy followed suit, but before either of them tasted a bite, the phone rang.

"Darn it!" She picked up the receiver. "Saddlers Prair—"

"This is Drew Dawson. I need to speak with Dr. Mark."

"Hi, Drew." Stacy glanced at Mark, who was chewing with a look of sheer pleasure on his face. "Aren't you supposed to bring Megan in shortly?"

"Put the doctor on the phone. Now."

Drew sounded tense. Frowning, Stacy handed the phone to Mark. "It's Drew Dawson."

Mark set his plate aside and took the phone. "Hey, Drew." He listened intently. "When did her water break? Has she had any contractions?"

Wishing she could hear Drew's replies, Stacy strained to listen.

"How far apart are they?" Mark asked, then nodded. "If

they're that close together, you don't have time to drive to the hospital or wait for an ambulance. I'll be right over. Yes, I know where you live. I'll call you from the road and tell you what I want you to do."

By the time he hung up, Stacy was already tacking her closing-early note on the clinic door.

"I'll drive," she offered, "and you concentrate on that call with Drew."

"Smart thinking."

Mark grabbed his medical bag and a few other supplies. Stacy switched the clinic phone to the answering service. She locked the door and within minutes they were speeding down the highway.

"She's thirty-six weeks along," Mark reassured Drew over the phone. "By now the baby's lungs are fully formed, and the rest of the organs are functional. Everything should be fine—provided you stay calm and listen."

He remained on the phone until Stacy turned into the ranch and rolled up the long drive. Before she even braked to a stop, Mrs. Ames, the housekeeper, opened the front door.

"They're upstairs and everything is ready for you. Hurry."

Medical bag in hand, Mark sprinted inside.

Not wanting to get in the way, Stacy followed at a slower pace.

"This is exciting," she said, greeting Mrs. Ames. "Does Jenny know?"

The housekeeper nodded. "School just let out, and she and Abby are on their way home. It happened really fast. One minute, Megan was helping me shell peas out back and talking about her doctor's appointment this afternoon. The next, her water broke. Luckily, Drew was on his way to the house to clean up and drive her to see Dr. Mark. Adam should be along soon."

A few moments later, Jenny and Abby raced inside, followed shortly by Adam. The little girl's eyes were huge.

"Isn't it exciting?" Jenny said, all but jumping up and down.

"Where's Drew?" Adam asked.

"Upstairs with Megan and Dr. Mark," Mrs. Ames said. "You all go sit in the den and I'll bring you something to eat."

Not being a family member, Stacy hesitated, but Jenny motioned her to follow.

Mrs. Ames delivered a platter of cold cuts and a plate of homemade cookies. As hungry as Stacy was and as tempting as the food looked, she couldn't eat a bite. Except for Abby, none of them could.

To pass the time, Jenny pulled out a board game to play with Abby, and invited Stacy, Adam and Mrs. Ames to join in. They tried, but no one could concentrate.

Adam paced the room. Abby kept running to the stairs and craning her neck upward. Mrs. Ames headed for the kitchen to make coffee, and Stacy and Jenny chatted quietly.

"We don't know if it's a boy or a girl," Jenny said.

"You're about to find out," Stacy said.

Standing behind Jenny, Adam massaged her shoulders. "As long as the baby is healthy, no one cares what they have." Fear and uncertainty darkened his face.

"At thirty-six weeks, the baby's lungs and other organs are mostly developed," Jenny said, repeating what Mark had told Drew. "The baby should be fine."

Everyone kept glancing at the wall clock. The minute hand *tick-tocked* softly, marking the passing time, which seemed to crawl by.

When Abby scampered to the bathroom, Jenny leaned forward and lowered her voice. "The baby's a month early, and no matter what you say about organ development at this stage, I can't help but be worried."

"Don't be—Mark is a skilled physician," Stacy assured her. "Megan and the baby are in the best possible hands."

She meant every word. She had no doubt that with Mark overseeing the birth, everything would be fine.

Chapter Fourteen

A scant twenty-five minutes after arriving at the house, Stacy heard the lusty cry of a newborn baby. "Did you hear that?" she said.

Mrs. Ames cocked an ear upward. "The baby has definitely arrived."

She hurried for the stairs, along with Jenny, Adam and Abby.

"Come on, Stacy!" Abby called out.

Stacy hesitated. This moment was special and private for the family. "I don't want to intrude."

Already partway up the stairs, Jenny stopped and looked down at her in surprise. "Are you kidding? The more, the merrier."

"Okay." Stacy followed the group toward Drew and Megan's bedroom at the end of the spacious hallway.

The door was closed, but excited and eager, they shamelessly eavesdropped.

"I can't hear anything," Jenny whispered. "The walls are too thick."

Too excited to hold still, Abby danced around. "A baby! A baby! Why don't they let us in? I want to meet my new baby cousin."

Jenny settled a calming hand on her shoulder. "They will, sweetie, they will."

Moments later, a jubilant-looking Drew opened the door.

"It's a boy," he said, a grin almost splitting his face. "A big, healthy boy. And he has the Dawson blue eyes."

Adam clapped him on the back. "Congrats, little brother. Now you can tell us the big secret you and Megan have kept all these months. What's his name?"

"Graham Nathan Dawson."

Mrs. Ames, who'd been with the family for decades, dabbed her eyes. "That's beautiful."

"Drew and Adam's father was Graham, and Nathan was their mother's maiden name," Jenny explained.

"Doc says everyone can come and meet him—you, too, Stacy."

Letting the family get the first look, Stacy hung back and peered from just inside the doorway at the tiny baby.

He was swaddled in a blanket, with only his little red face visible. His features were slightly squashed from the birth, but otherwise he was perfect. Awed, she couldn't look away.

Longing swept through her for a baby of her own. Followed by doubts that she'd ever find the right man to have a child with. But this was no time for self-pity.

Mark joined her, his expression pleased. Together they watched the Dawson family, vicariously sharing their joy. Stacy's heart filled with feelings too big to contain. Without thinking, she grabbed for Mark's hand.

He looked surprised, but his grip tightened around hers. They stayed that way for some time, then at the same instant, let go.

"Do they need to get to the hospital?" she asked in a low voice.

He shook his head and raised his voice so that everyone could hear. "It was an easy birth, and the baby looks good. His Apgar score is a ten. That's perfect, and means he's healthy."

"That's my boy," Drew said.

"I'll still need to come back tomorrow to check on him and give him a routine blood test."

"You'd come back here for that?" Drew asked.

"I don't expect a mom who just gave birth to make a trip out so soon."

Drew and the rest of the family looked impressed. "That's going above and beyond, Doc. You're the best."

"You are," Megan said, smiling. "After Drew and our son."

"He has lots of hair," Abby said wonderingly. "Can I touch it?"

"Sure," Drew said. "If you wash your hands, you can even hold him for a minute."

Abby raced for the bathroom, the rest of the family following.

"We should've had the baby shower last weekend," Stacy teased. "I'll let Carol and Louisa know it's cancelled, and I'll bring your gift over this weekend."

"That'd be great," Megan said. "I really don't mind missing my shower. Having Graham trumps everything else." She looked exhausted, but radiant. "You can hold him, too, Stacy."

"Really?" Stacy smiled. "Then I'd better wash my hands, as well. I'll be right back."

When she returned to the bedroom, Abby was seated in an armchair, cradling the baby and staring at him in wonder. "He's sleeping," she told Stacy.

"I see that."

"Everyone else has held him," Jenny said, taking Graham from Abby. "It's your turn now, Stacy."

Stacy sat down in the armchair and Jenny handed her the baby.

He weighed nothing. His rosebud mouth formed a tiny O, and suddenly his very blue eyes opened and looked directly into Stacy's. Feelings flooded her—warmth, love and a fierce tenderness.

"Stacy, are you crying?" Jenny asked.

She nodded. "I don't know why. He's just so beautiful."

After murmurs of agreement from everyone, Megan looked longingly at her son. "May I have him back now?" she asked.

With a tender look, Drew collected his son and gently placed him beside Megan.

"Megan and Graham worked hard," Mark said. "They need their rest."

After kissing his wife's forehead, Drew herded everyone out.

Downstairs, the group entered the living room.

"Ready to go?" Mark asked Stacy.

"Don't leave just yet," Drew said. "Please stay and have a celebratory drink with the family."

Mark glanced at Stacy, and she nodded her okay.

"We'd enjoy that," he said.

Drew poured champagne for everyone but Abby. Mrs. Ames opened a bottle of sparkling cider for the little girl. They raised their glasses.

Adam spoke first. "Congratulations, Drew. I'm proud of you and Megan for giving me a nephew."

"We had a good time doing it," Drew quipped.

Everyone laughed.

"My turn." Drew tilted his flute toward Mark. "To Dr. Mark."

Mark dipped his head, just as he did whenever a patient complimented him. Unlike many doctors, he wasn't at all egotistical. And yet he was extremely competent and talented. Better even than Dr. Tom.

Stacy's heart filled with pride, along with a warmth that was dangerously close to love. After fighting her feelings for days, she had to admit she was half in love with Mark Engle. A love that could go nowhere. She stifled a sigh.

"We really owe you, man," Drew went on. "I hate like hell that you're leaving Saddlers Prairie."

"I appreciate that," Mark said.

Despite the smile on his lips, his expression shifted subtly. Something a person wouldn't notice unless she knew him well.

Mark was torn about leaving.

Stacy caught her breath. Was there a chance he might change his mind and stay, or was that the wishful thinking of her yearning heart?

BY THE TIME MRS. AMES SHUT the door behind Mark and Stacy, the sun was starting its drop toward the horizon.

"That was such a cool experience," Stacy gushed as they ambled toward her car.

She seemed more relaxed than she'd been in days, and definitely warmer toward him, Mark thought. That could be from the champagne, though she *had* grabbed his hand long before the toasts.

He'd been surprised and touched that she'd initiated the physical connection with him. Especially after the distance between them the past few days.

Stacy fumbled as she got the keys from her handbag.

"You've had a few glasses of champagne," he said. "Why don't I drive."

"That's a very good idea." She dropped the keys into his palm.

Before he was halfway down the long driveway, she turned in her seat. "What you did in there was amazing," she said, looking awed.

Mark's heart swelled with pride and other feelings he wasn't about to examine. He shrugged. "Megan and Mother

Nature did most of the work. But the whole thing *was* pretty special. I've never delivered a baby in someone's home."

Or spent a few hours celebrating with the ebullient relatives. Mark had enjoyed that. He liked Drew and Adam, liked Jenny, Abby and Mrs. Ames, too.

"I haven't, either," Stacy said. "Dr. Tom has done lots of home deliveries, but I've never gone along. With the hospital so far away, there isn't always time to get there before a birth. If you stayed in Saddlers Prairie, you'd have plenty more opportunities like today."

She clapped her hand over her mouth. "Did I just say that? Oops. Next time, remind me to stop at one glass of champagne." She laughed, then broke off. "But you won't be here next time."

Will you?

She didn't voice the words. Didn't need to. Her questioning look was loud and clear.

For a few minutes in the Dawsons' living room, Mark had actually considered sticking around. He'd felt so comfortable and gratified, and he knew that if he stayed, the Dawson family would become lifelong friends.

But that was crazy, and he was damned if he'd deviate from the plan that had steered him so well. He was *not* staying in Saddlers Prairie. He was going to L.A. to take a great job, make money and eventually buy into a lucrative partnership. Period.

"The Dawsons are good people," he said, neatly changing the subject.

"The best, and so *open*. Including me in their celebration and letting me hold Graham…I'll never forget that."

Neither would Mark. Seeing Stacy with the tiny newborn in her arms, her beautiful face transformed with elation and wonder and tenderness… The image like that would be forever imprinted in his brain.

He could easily picture her cradling her own child.

His child. *Theirs.*

Where had *that* thought come from?

Aside from the fact that he was leaving town soon, he wasn't ready for marriage, let alone a baby. Right now, he wanted to focus on his career.

"Do you want kids someday?" he asked, all the same.

"At least two," Stacy replied without hesitation. "How about you?"

"In the distant future—after I establish myself in L.A."

"You mean, after you're rich."

"Something like that."

In the few beats of silence that fell between them, a pair of meadowlarks winged past the car.

Stacy sighed. "Men are lucky. They don't have that biological ticking clock."

"You're only thirty, Stace. You have time."

"I guess so."

With her head down and her hair curtaining her face, Mark couldn't see her expression. He had no idea what she was thinking, but at least they were talking.

"The past few days have been… That's no way to…" Stumbling for the right words, he cleared his throat and tried again. "What I'm trying to say is, I want us to be comfortable around each other."

Stacy angled her head at him. "Me, too."

"If I swear to keep my hands to myself, can we start over?"

"I'd like that," she said, almost shyly.

Feeling as if a ten-pound boulder had rolled off his shoulders, Mark smiled. "We just shared something very special, and I'm in no mood to spend the evening alone. I happen to have a couple of steaks sitting in the fridge. Why don't I grill them for dinner? Then we'll dig into that pie we never had the chance to enjoy."

"I'd forgotten all about that delicious pie." She hesitated, hands twisting in her lap. "But I don't know."

Mark's gut twisted right along with them. But he meant what he'd said. He and Stacy had shared in the miracle of birth and tonight he wanted her company. Anything physical was out.

"Hey, we're starting over, remember?" He was not going to blow this. It all boiled down to the control he was so good at. If she stayed for dinner, he wouldn't lay a finger on her, would act the perfect gentleman.

"Besides, you can't drive yourself home until you sober up," he added. "I have it on the word of a doctor who knows, food will help. What do you say?" Not sure why this was so important, he sucked in a breath.

After a moment, Stacy nodded. "All right, I'll come for dinner, but only if you let me help cook."

Mark exhaled. "It's a deal."

STILL FEELING THE CHAMPAGNE, Stacy shook her head at the steaks Mark had taken from the refrigerator.

"Those things are so big, they'll barely fit on the hibachi. As hungry as I am—and I'm starving—I'll never be able to eat all that."

"Yeah, but think of the leftovers. Steak and eggs, steak sandwich, steak hash." Mark licked his lips, and Stacy laughed.

"You're making me even hungrier." She filled the pot he'd given her to boil the potatoes.

"Hungrier is good."

He flashed an irresistible grin without a hint of sexual innuendo, when Stacy was all but panting for him. The emotions she'd tamped down the past few days had flared up at the Dawsons' ranch and burned ever since.

Afraid she'd somehow give away her feelings, she focused

on peeling the potatoes. Mark had once again become the charmer he was before, yet he was different in ways she couldn't quite put her finger on. She only knew that their relationship had somehow changed.

Her feelings for him had deepened. She wasn't sure if he could say the same. Since leaving the ranch, he'd gone out of his way to make her feel comfortable and safe, acting as if he no longer desired her.

That was probably a good thing, because if he were to touch her this very moment, she was sure to burst into flames. For her heart's sake, she couldn't let that happen.

"Speaking of empty bellies, I think I'll check the coals." He wandered to the open window and peered down.

Stacy admitted that she was also puzzled. Could his feelings for her change so quickly?

Well, he had said that he wanted to start over.

If only she could convince her heart to do the same.

Mark turned from the window. "The coals look ready." He grabbed the steak platter and a pair of tongs. "I'll take these babies downstairs."

"And I'll make the salad."

As soon as he left, Stacy plunked onto a stool at the eating bar. She glanced around Dr. Tom's compact but organized kitchen. The doctor enjoyed cooking and had acquired cutting-edge appliances and equipment she envied.

She also enjoyed cooking whenever time allowed. She imagined Mark pulling steaks from *her* refrigerator to grill in *her* backyard.

What would her life be like if they shared dinner every night? If he also shared her bed?

Yearning flooded her, making her weak with need. Stacy frowned. "Stop it right now."

Mark was leaving. After their discussion on the drive home, she was convinced he'd never consider living in Saddlers Prairie. He'd jump right into his new job and lifestyle, and in no time Stacy and this small Montana town would be distant blips in his memory.

The maudlin thoughts made her want to cry. She really needed to sober up. She filled a glass with water and sipped it while she gathered ingredients for the salad. By the time she finished, the potatoes were ready and the mouthwatering aroma of sizzling steaks wafted through the open window.

"Hey, Stace," Mark called from the front yard.

She headed for the window and looked down. Cooking tongs in hand, head cocked back, he stared up at her. Grinning, handsome and oh, so appealing. Even in the dusk, she swore she saw the crinkles at the corners of his eyes.

Her wayward heart beat a little faster. "You rang?" she teased.

"How about a picnic out here?"

Dining with the sunset as background sounded far too romantic. She preferred to eat up here, where the lights were nice and bright. "It'll be dark soon," she said. "Besides, where would we sit?"

"We'll turn on the floodlights, and I'll drag out the table and chairs from the downstairs kitchen. What do you say?"

His pleading look was impossible to ignore. She laughed. "I say, we're having a picnic."

Chapter Fifteen

This was a night for lovers, Mark thought—which left him and Stacy out. Any sexual hunger was off-limits and his libido firmly under wraps. As difficult as corralling his feelings was, the effort was well worth the trouble, for once again Stacy seemed content and comfortable.

She sat across from him at the little café table he'd hauled outside. Easy conversation and the clink of cutlery against plates floated pleasantly through the night air.

Beyond the reach of the floodlights, darkness cloaked everything, accompanied by a stillness so deep that when silence fell between them, he heard his own blood rush through his ears.

"Tell me what you do around here when you aren't at the clinic or digging in your garden," he said over coffee and slices of Opal Farraday's excellent pie.

"You know about the book club," she said. "I also knit and like to get together with friends. Now and then, if the weather behaves and I have the time, I enjoy exploring the prairie. This time of year, there are so many things to see— wildflowers, birds and who knows what other treasures hidden in the tall grass. I also love to cook, especially for other people."

"Then by all means, invite me to dinner," he said. Partly

to tease and partly because having tasted those buttery garlic mashed potatoes, he wanted to sample more of her cooking.

"All right, I will. How about Saturday night, around six?"

"That's Memorial Day weekend," he reminded her, thinking she might have plans over the holiday.

"Outside of stopping by the Dawsons' Saturday morning with a baby blanket, I'm not going anywhere."

"Then it's a date," Mark said. Only, they weren't dating. "That is, it's a—"

"Payback dinner invitation."

Her smile told him she understood, and he let out a silent breath of relief. "You were telling me what you do to entertain yourself around here," he reminded her.

"The garden takes a huge amount of time, especially in the spring and summer. Right now, things are starting to grow, and I spend most evenings outside. If you saw my backyard, you'd understand. It's huge and mostly garden, and I'm continually fighting the weeds. They're much hardier than the flowers and vegetables, with a longer growing season."

Looking as if she were about to confess a secret, she leaned toward him. "This is going to sound weird, but I really don't mind. Weeding relaxes me, just like working on that old Mustang did."

"Interesting," Mark said. "I've never lived in a place with a yard, and I've never pulled a single weed."

Stacy rested her chin on her fist. "Sure you have. You pull the weeds from your patients every day—metaphorically speaking."

He tipped his coffee mug toward her. "Clever, Miss Andrews."

"Thank you, Dr. Engle."

They smiled at each other, then tucked into their pie in companionable silence.

When Stacy finished, she sat back in her chair and groaned.

"I can't believe I ate almost my entire steak *and* the huge slice of pie you cut for me. I'm definitely sober now, but I think I might pop."

She really did look glutted, and Mark couldn't stop a chuckle. "Don't worry, the feeling will pass. Just think, tomorrow morning you'll wake up hungry all over again."

Her nose wrinkled, making her look cute. "At the moment, I can't even imagine breakfast. I'm not used to eating so much."

"You deserved this meal. We both did. We worked hard today."

"*You* did," she corrected.

"So did you. You managed the clinic all day, then drove me to the Dawsons' and stuck around. Plus you made the salad and those great mashed potatoes. That counts as work."

"Don't forget eating. That takes a lot of energy, too."

Her eyes flashed humor—and something else that was soft and warm.

Desire hit Mark hard. He glanced away. Stacy suddenly seemed to find her napkin fascinating.

He ought to call an end to the evening now, before he ruined everything by doing something dumb and kissing her again. The second they finished their coffees, tonight was over. He'd make sure of that.

"I may have a yard in L.A. someday, but I won't take up gardening," he said, reminding them both that he was leaving soon. "I plan to use my free time exploring, taking in shows and trying out restaurants. In a big city like L.A., there are plenty of options. But you know that."

Stacy placidly stirred her coffee. "I'm sure you'll have a wonderful time."

Her expression never changed, yet somehow, the air was now charged with the same tension that had plagued them the past few days.

Confused and filled with dread, Mark frowned. "Everything all right?"

"Absolutely," she replied a little too breezily.

"Look, just because we started over tonight doesn't mean we have to agree on everything." Determined to regain the easiness between them, he gave her a friendly smile. "I know what you think of L.A., but I'm eager to live there."

"Yes, I know." She stacked the plates, then pushed her chair back and stood. "It's getting late, and I should leave soon."

Mark jumped up and nudged her gently aside. "You don't have to help with the cleanup."

"I want to."

Upstairs, he rinsed the dishes, which Stacy silently loaded into the dishwasher. He wished she'd relax again, but knew he couldn't force her to do so.

"Thanks, Stace," he said when the job was done.

"Don't thank me yet," she said. "We still have the potato pot, the mixer and the other things that won't fit into the dishwasher."

She was still way too stiff. In a burst of inspiration, Mark glanced at her feet. "I keep meaning to tell you that I like those red ladybugs on the green background. You do that a lot, paint interesting stuff on your toenails."

"You noticed." She actually smiled, and his responding grin was pure relief.

"That's another thing I like to do in my spare time— change the colors and designs on my toenails. Especially in sandal weather. It's fun and not difficult—as long as Smooth Talker doesn't blurt out some dirty word while I'm painting." She laughed.

The warmth of a smile lingered on her lips, and Mark wanted her all over again.

She caught him staring at her mouth. Her expression sobered and unmistakable yearning clouded her eyes. Her dark lashes fluttered against her cheeks before she pivoted toward the sink.

Battling the raging need to haul her close and finish what they'd started days ago, he clenched his hands at his sides. "I'll finish the rest myself," he said through gritted teeth.

This time Stacy didn't argue. He followed her down the stairs.

"What about the table and chairs?" she asked as she stepped outside. "Let me at least bring in the chairs."

Just leave, he silently commanded. *Before I do something that will ruin everything.* "I'll take care of them."

She frowned. "If that's what you want."

What he wanted was Stacy naked and hungry under him.

"Thanks again for dinner," she said.

He gave a terse nod.

He didn't draw in an easy breath again until her car left the parking lot and turned onto the road.

"HAVE MARK'S EARS BEEN ringing?" Jenny asked Stacy when she stopped by Saturday morning to deliver the baby blanket. Drew, Megan and Graham were catching up on sleep with a morning nap, Adam was out doing chores and Abby was upstairs in her room. "We sang his praises on Wednesday, but when he came back Thursday with a rattle for Graham and a whistle for Abby... Our entire family is in love with him. That man is a keeper."

Didn't Stacy know it. Though he hadn't mentioned the gifts he'd brought for Graham and Abby when he'd returned to the ranch to administer the blood test. In so many ways, he was thoughtful and considerate, both as a man and a physician.

"He's definitely special," she said as Jenny walked her to

her car. Unable to hold in her feelings, she added, "Can I tell you something in confidence?"

"Always. Let me guess—you and Mark are seeing each other outside the clinic."

Stacy puzzled over her friend's canny remark. "How could you possibly know that?"

"The way you looked at each other after Graham was born—your feelings for each other were pretty obvious."

"We aren't exactly dating, Jenny. Other than that awful dinner at the mayor's, we've seen each other outside the office exactly twice."

"Has he kissed you again?"

"And more." Lowering her voice, Stacy told her friend everything—about running into Mark at Val and Silas's barbecue, the steamy make-out session that followed on the hood of Mark's car and their run-in with the sheriff. "Gabe promised not to say anything," she finished.

"As far as I know, he hasn't." Jenny shaded her eyes against the sun. "I haven't heard a word until now."

Stacy felt relieved. "It's a good thing Gabe came along before Mark and I got too carried away. Mark has no plans to ever come back to Saddlers Prairie, and when we talked the next day, I let him know that I couldn't let our physical relationship go any further. We haven't gone near each other since."

Jenny gave her a sympathetic look. "That's got to be difficult for you both."

"It hasn't been easy. Still, I thought everything was under control—until we left your house the afternoon Graham was born. That was a powerful experience for both Mark and me, and neither of us wanted to spend our evening alone. We ended up having dinner together at Mark's."

"Ah." Jenny's knowing expression spoke volumes.

Stacy shook her head. "I meant what I said—nothing happened. But I wanted it to," she admitted.

"Hi, Stacy!" Abby called from the doorway. "Mama, I need you inside."

"She has a playdate soon," Jenny said. "Don't leave just yet. I'll be right back."

While Stacy waited for her friend to return, she thought about how Mark wanted to start over. He'd been sweet and relaxed during dinner, without a hint of sexual desire toward her. The conversation had flowed easily—until the end of the meal.

The mention of L.A. had put a damper on the evening, at least for Stacy. From that moment on, the easiness between them had vanished.

Then cleaning up in the kitchen… The raw hunger glinting in Mark's eyes had ravaged her self-control. One touch, one kiss, and she'd have been lost.

But instead of kissing her, he'd turned downright rude and had practically kicked her out, making her wonder if she merely *wanted* him to desire her again.

Since then, their relationship had felt tentative and shaky, less tense than before Graham's birth, but not as warm and wonderful as during the dinner that had followed. They'd both been careful to stick to work-related issues, doctor to office manager.

Jenny emerged from the house. "Sorry about that. Abby's gathering up the toys she wants to bring to her playdate. Now, about you and Mark. Since he *is* leaving exactly one week from today, keeping your distance is probably for the best."

"Believe me, I know. Still, all I think about is making love with him." Stacy had never wanted a man so much, not even in the early days with Vince. "You don't understand how difficult it is."

"You forget, I went through a similar situation with Adam."

"But you two ended up married. Mark has his life plan all laid out, and for now, marriage isn't a part of it."

"Plans aren't set in concrete. You never know—he could change his mind. Especially if your feelings for each other are strong enough."

"He definitely likes me, but he wants the salary, prestige and future partnership more." Stacy bit her lip. "I probably shouldn't have invited him to dinner tonight." She was amazed that he hadn't cancelled. "Do you think he'll make a move, and what should I do if he does?"

For a few seconds, her friend simply studied her. "What do *you* want?"

Stacy didn't have to stop and think about the answer. "I want Mark."

"Then follow your heart. Don't worry about the future, just stay in the present, focus on the now and let the evening unfold."

Stacy wasn't sure what she'd expected from her friend, but it wasn't this. "You really think I should?"

"If—"

"I'm ready, Mama!" Abby bounded out the door with several toys.

Conversation at an end, Stacy waved at the little girl. "Bye, Abby, and have fun."

"You have fun, too!"

On the way to the family car, Jenny glanced over her shoulder. "Call me and let me know how it goes."

As STACY CLEANED AND cooked on Saturday afternoon, Jenny's advice stayed with her. So did the conversation with Connie Volles, a cashier at Spenser's who was about Stacy's age.

"Having someone special over for dinner?" Connie had asked as she rang up Stacy's groceries.

Not wanting to air her personal life to the chatty checker, Stacy had hedged. "What makes you think so?"

"Expensive wine, two Cornish game hens, baking chocolate, lady fingers and whipping cream…. Looks like a romantic evening to me."

Worried that she might be making a statement tonight that she didn't want to make, Stacy had frowned. "Do you think it's *too* romantic?"

"That all depends." Connie had lowered her voice. "Are you cooking for Dr. Mark?"

Stacy's furious blush had given her away, and the checker had nodded knowingly. "Thought so."

"Don't go getting any ideas, Connie. A week from today, he leaves for L.A."

"I wouldn't bet on that. You're an attractive woman, and he's not blind. Add in that dinner you're cooking and the wine, and it's going to be a *very* special night." Connie spread her palm over her chest and smiled. "Dr. Mark could easily change his mind."

Jenny had said the same thing, but Stacy knew he wouldn't. "Trust me, he won't."

"Miracles do happen." When Stacy snorted, Connie held up her crossed fingers. "I'll keep them crossed all night."

Miracles do happen. Stacy didn't believe that for one second, yet the words had stayed with her all day.

Hope stirred in her, along with a fine current of anticipation. She called herself a silly fool, yet kept right on anticipating.

Late that afternoon, Stacy checked the house with a critical eye. Everything was neat and clean. Some of the flowers had finally bloomed and a colorful bouquet filled a crystal vase on the living-room coffee table. The dining room was set with her favorite placemats and a centerpiece of more flowers.

The Cornish hens sat in a pan on the counter, stuffed and ready to bake. Appetizers, the wine and a rich, chocolate icebox cake waited in the refrigerator.

All was ready. Except for her. She drew a lilac bubble bath and sank into it, soaking the edge off her thrumming nerves. She painted her toenails purple with tiny yellow stars and paid more attention than usual to her makeup.

Fifteen minutes before she expected Mark, Stacy slipped into the sexy sundress that had tempted him before, then fixed her hair using his barrettes.

"Awk, pretty woman," Smooth Talker crooned in a velvety voice.

"Thanks, ST. Promise me you'll behave tonight."

The bird cocked his head coyly.

At a quarter to six, Stacy slipped the Cornish hens into the oven and started a Colbie Caillat album on the iPod. She set out the appetizers and uncorked the wine to let it air. Then she sat down to wait.

At five after six, she shrugged. No one showed up exactly on time. By six-fifteen, she started to worry.

"ST wants love," the parrot squawked.

"So do I," Stacy said.

ST opened his vivid red beak and snatched the treat Stacy held between her fingers. Absently, she stroked his head and contemplated what to do if Mark didn't come.

"Awk! Look sharp, look sharp!" the parrot squawked, meaning company had arrived.

Relief flooded her. Seconds later, the doorbell rang. "Remember—behave yourself," she reminded Smooth Talker.

Not wanting to look anxious, she smoothed her dress and checked her hair, then made herself wait another few seconds before she sauntered to the door.

Chapter Sixteen

Coming to Stacy's house for dinner wasn't exactly the smartest move Mark had ever made. Yet here he was, waiting for her to let him in. She seemed to be taking her sweet time.

Then the door swung open. "Hi," she said, lifting one delicate eyebrow.

"Sorry I'm late." In an effort to keep his cool about tonight, he'd pulled up the map Cody had emailed for tomorrow's hike and pored over it, temporarily losing track of the time.

"No problem."

She wore a sexy smile, the braless dress that made his mouth go dry, and red, strappy heels Mark had never seen. Her lips were the same red, only shiny. She smelled great, too, like a gardenia.

Mark knew he was in trouble, and decided that stuffing a handful of condoms in his pocket earlier had probably been a good idea. Every instinct warned him to turn around and get out of here, but his feet remained solidly planted on her welcome mat. He cleared his throat. "You look amazing."

"Awk, shut your trap, you two-fisted shit bastard," a loud voice scolded from inside.

Mark started. "Let me guess—that's Smooth Talker."

"Yes, and after he promised to behave." Stacy laughed. "Come in and meet him."

The brightly colored bird stood on a perch in front of

the living-room window. So as not to startle him, Mark approached slowly and kept his voice low. "Hey there, ST, I'm Mark."

The parrot blinked, then sidestepped along his perch to move as far away from Mark as possible.

"Hmm." Stacy frowned. "Feed him a treat and he'll probably relax."

She placed a walnut-size seed ball in the palm of Mark's hand. He held out the offering, but the parrot ignored him. "I don't think he likes me," he said.

"At least he's not yelling at you. Don't pay any attention to him and eventually he'll warm up to you. Please, sit down."

Mark nodded. "I brought you something." He handed her the gift he'd picked up earlier at a bookstore near the hospital.

"What's this?"

"The other night you said you liked to explore the prairie and see the plants and animals. This is a book about the wildflowers and birds in Montana."

"I've been meaning to buy something like this, but now I don't have to. Thanks, Mark."

She clasped the book to her perfect breasts. Mark envied that book.

"This is a nice house," he said, taking a comfy-looking chair.

"Now it is, but you should've seen the place when I bought it. Every wall was an awful mustard-yellow, and the carpets were the color of split-pea soup. The men who replaced the carpet said they'd never seen such a hideous color."

"Sounds pretty bad," he said.

"Awful. Would you like to try my eggplant dip? You eat it with pita chips."

"Thanks."

Stacy leaned toward him with the appetizer tray. The top of her dress gaped open a fraction, allowing Mark a tempting peek at the creamy tops of her breasts. Breasts he knew the feel and taste of. Breasts unbound by any bra.

His body stirred, and for the second time, he cleared his throat. "Something smells good."

"Cornish game hens."

She poured them both a glass of wine, then sat down opposite the coffee table and crossed her long legs. The skirt of her dress rode up her thighs. Not quite as high as Mark wanted, but enough to get him even more hot and bothered. Shifting in his seat, he willed his body to behave.

"I saw Tom this afternoon," he said in an effort to control himself.

Stacy nodded. "I haven't talked to him today, but I am planning to visit sometime tomorrow. How was he?"

"Antsy to leave. He put his name in at a retirement community outside town. They have an available apartment and are getting it ready now."

"He never said a word to me—he's going to hear about that!" Stacy sipped her wine. "I guess this means he really is retiring. That's a huge relief."

She didn't bring up the subject of his replacement, and neither did Mark.

She uncrossed her legs, helped herself to an appetizer, then crossed them again. The skirt rode up a little higher. She popped the pita chip into her mouth, closed her eyes and made a sound of pleasure. Killing him.

If she kept this up, he'd be too embarrassed to move from the chair. "I'd like to see that backyard garden you mentioned," he said.

"I'd love to show it to you. Follow me."

She led Mark through sliding-glass doors off a cozy dining room that could've been set for dinner. He wasn't sure—too busy watching Stacy's hips sway and the tempting curve of her behind.

The large yard was surrounded by a natural wood privacy fence. The garden took up a good two-thirds of the area. Mark smelled flowers and, though it was early in the growing season, the pungent scent of herbs.

"This is some garden," he said. "No wonder you spend so much time weeding."

"Didn't I tell you? The herbs and vegetables are on the left, and the flowers are on the right. I wish the peas and beans were ready so I could serve them tonight, but they need a good month yet."

The wind tousled her hair, but thanks to the barrettes Mark had given her, none of the strands ended up in her eyes.

"I really like these clips," she said, her smile sweet with appreciation.

Feelings Mark didn't understand crowded his chest, and his hunger for her intensified. Swallowing, he shaded his eyes against the slanting sun and surveyed the freshly mowed grass.

A beeper sounded, and Stacy glanced over her shoulder at the house. "That's the timer. I need to get a few things ready before we eat."

"I'll help."

"That'd be great. You can dress the salad."

She started toward the sliding doors, her hair swishing and those hips swaying. God help him, he reached out and clasped her smooth, bare shoulders. She froze.

"Stacy. Turn around and look at me."

Wordless, she complied. Sooty lashes framed her impossibly blue eyes. Eyes a man could drown in.

"I lied the other day," he said. "I care about you, Stacy, and I don't want to start over."

"You don't?" Tiny lines formed between her eyebrows. "Then what *do* you want, Mark?"

"To taste you everywhere." He ran his thumb over her

full lower lip, gratified when her mouth opened a fraction. "I want to make you moan with pleasure while I make slow, passionate love with you. I've wanted that since the day we first met." He dropped his hand. "But I'm leaving, and I know that means you—"

"Shh." She placed her finger to his lips, gently silencing him. "What if I told you I don't care if you're leaving, that tonight I want exactly the same thing as you—for us to be together."

The words almost brought him to his knees. "You don't want that. You want a real relationship."

Stacy wet her lips. "Tonight, all I care about is us together."

Mark caught his breath. "You're saying—"

"I'm saying," she said, twining her arms around his neck, "make love with me, Mark."

A strangled sound rumbled from his throat. He wrapped his arms around her, pulling her against his hungry body. Softness and curves against hard angles.

Nothing tender in this kiss. Stacy responded with an eagerness that drowned out every logical thought in his head, a long, passionate melding of mouths that urged him to pull her down right here on the grass and take her.

With effort, he broke away and grabbed her hand. "Let's go inside."

THE SECOND MARK PULLED Stacy through the sliding doors, he kissed her again. More deeply and urgently than she could ever remember being kissed. Grasping her bottom, anchoring her against his erection.

Need settled achingly between her legs, and she molded herself to him.

After a frustratingly short while, he stilled. "The damned timer's still buzzing."

"I'd better turn everything off." Dragging herself from the

heaven of his arms, Stacy moved dazedly toward the kitchen. She silenced the timer, turned off the oven and cracked open the door.

She was about to slide mitts on her hands and remove the hens, when Mark grasped her hips from behind.

"They'll keep," he growled, holding her so that her bottom fit against his rigid groin.

Stacy tried to turn in his arms and kiss him, but he anchored her where she was. He nuzzled the sensitive crook of her shoulder, then ran his tongue up the column of her neck. Caught hold of her earlobe with his teeth and tugged gently.

Shivers of desire made her tremble. "Please, Mark," she said, struggling to face him.

"Where's the bedroom?" he asked, sounding hoarse and winded.

"Down…" He palmed her breasts through her dress, and she had difficulty focusing. "Down the hall, and up the stairs."

At last, he turned her in his arms and kissed her soundly. One kiss led to another, their mouths wet and exploring. Mark's hands were everywhere, setting her on fire.

Eager to touch him, as well, she tore at the buttons on the placket of his shirt. As soon as she finished, he shrugged out of it. Stacy slid her hands over the light smattering of hair on his chest and felt his muscles tense. She ran her palms down his tight belly, toward his waistband.

Sucking in a sharp breath, Mark circled her wrists and pulled her eager fingers away.

"But I want to touch you," she said.

"And I want to finish inside you, understand?" He grabbed her hand and tugged her toward the stairs.

Seconds later, they entered the loft. "Now, where were we?" he said. He kissed her again, then slid her dress over her head. With a soft whish, it fell to the floor. Feeling oddly shy, Stacy stood before him dressed only in panties and shoes.

Mark devoured her with his gaze. "Red bikini panties that match your shoes—dear God, you're sexy. I want you so much."

"I want you, too." Emboldened by the raw hunger in his eyes, she stroked his rigid length through his khakis. "These pants must go."

"Ladies first."

With Mark avidly watching, Stacy stepped out of her shoes, then removed her panties. Moments later, his pants and shorts followed.

He was gloriously naked, handsome and hard and so very beautiful. Stacy's heart overflowed with emotion. With love. She barely had time to register her feelings and remind herself that nothing mattered but *now,* before Mark tugged her toward the bed.

As he jerked off the spread and tossed it aside, a thought suddenly occurred to her. "What about protection?" she asked, silently kicking herself for forgetting something so important.

Mark gave her a sheepish look. "I brought condoms with me tonight, just in case." He grabbed several from his pants pocket and tossed them onto the bedside table.

"Hey, you need *one* of those now," Stacy reminded him.

"Not just yet. First I intend to get to know every inch of your body." His smoldering glance turned her bones to liquid. "Lie back, Stace."

He started with her eyelids, gently kissing them closed. He kissed the tip of her nose, then took her mouth with a savage intensity that left her gasping and hungry. Slowly and thoroughly, he traveled down her body, licking and nipping and tasting, until she thought she was sure to incinerate.

Then he was kneeling between her legs, blowing softly

on the part of her that most craved his attention. He didn't touch, though, making her restless and wild with need. Tensing, Stacy lifted her hips. "Mark, please," she begged.

"Is this what you want?" He opened her with his fingers, and his tongue flicked the most sensitive part of her body.

Finally. Stacy moaned.

He knew what he was doing. Probing, stroking, touching her in exactly the way she wanted, right…there. He flicked the sensitive spot again. Stacy tensed. The third time, she shattered.

When she collapsed limply against the sheets and opened her eyes, he was propped up on his elbows, looking pleased with himself.

"I enjoyed that," he said.

"Me, too."

She glanced at the erection jutting from his groin. "Now it's my turn. On your back, Doctor."

Eager to oblige, Mark settled against the pillow, hands behind his head, and let Stacy explore.

After kissing his mouth, she licked his flat nipples. Mark made a sound of pleasure and felt her lips curl into a smile against his chest.

She traveled lower, taking an agonizingly long time to get to where he really wanted her. She paused to trace his navel with her tongue, and his breath hissed.

"Am I hurting you?" she asked, a teasing light in her eyes.

"Oh, yeah, but in a very good way. Don't stop."

She continued toward his groin. Knowing what was coming, Mark gripped the sheets. Her tongue slid over his length, giving a pleasure so keen his eyes watered. She was so beautiful, so damn… Mark groaned.

About to lose control, he flipped her over. "Now I'm ready for that condom."

In seconds, he sheathed himself. Stacy was waiting, her

arms open and welcoming. He held her close, the tip of his erection grazing her passage in sweet torture.

Gripping his hips with her thighs, she tugged him still closer. "I need you *now*."

In one long, slick thrust, he entered her fully.

She cried out.

Mark froze. "Too fast?"

"No—perfect."

Taking her mouth in a deep kiss, he pulled back so that he almost left her, then slowly eased all the way in again. He intended to keep the same rhythm, make her beg for more. But she squeezed her muscles hard around him and he lost himself and gave in to the primal urge that pulsed within him.

He thrust deeply. Then again, harder and faster until she moaned and convulsed, bringing him to a swift climax. Sweet, sweet release.

Afterward, he held her close, cradled against his side.

She kissed his rib cage, then let out a contented sigh. "That was the best sex I've ever had."

"Me, too."

His chest swelled with feelings he wasn't about to explore. Lust, he assured himself. Already he wanted her again. On the heels of the thought, his stomach growled.

"That sounded pitiful," Stacy said. "I think it's time to feed you."

"Awk, you shit bastard traitor, she's mine!" Smooth Talker cried when they descended the stairs and neared the living room.

"He sounds jealous." Mark put his arm around Stacy. "She's mine, buddy. Go find someone of your own species."

"He needs to go to sleep. Bedtime, ST," Stacy crooned as she placed the bird in his cage and covered him for the night.

They ate in the dining room, Mark in his pants, and Stacy wearing her panties and his shirt with the sleeves rolled up.

It was way too big for her, which somehow made her look sexy as hell.

With her hair every which way, her lips slightly swollen from kisses and her skin still flushed with arousal, she was the most beautiful woman Mark had ever known. He swallowed back a wave of tenderness that scared him witless.

"You don't like your chicken." Stacy frowned. "It is a little dried out."

"It's delicious," Mark said. "But even if it were burned to a crisp and we had nothing to eat tonight, making love with you would be worth it."

Her warm, intimate smile was only for him. His heart thudded in his chest, his groin stirred with fresh desire, and he forgot about everything but the sensuous woman across the table.

Somehow he finished the meal without rounding the table, hauling her close and slaking his body's hunger. Stacy seemed oblivious.

"I made a chocolate icebox cake. Would you like dessert now or later?" she asked, pushing the hair from her eyes.

"Now, and I'm not talking cake."

He held out his hand and led her from the table, back up the stairs to the bedroom. This time they made love slowly and tenderly, Mark giving pleasure until Stacy writhed and moaned and pleaded. Only then did he slip on a condom and satisfy them both.

Not long after they finished, Stacy fell asleep. Mark lay beside her, staring at the dark ceiling and wondering just what in the hell he was doing, sleeping in her bed when he was leaving town soon.

Chapter Seventeen

Stacy woke up to sunlight streaming through a crack in the drapes. Tired—she and Mark hadn't slept much—and sated from a night of unforgettable lovemaking, she smiled and turned over to greet him. His side of the bed was empty.

He was gone, without even a goodbye.

Her heart stuttered in her chest. Then she heard the water running, followed by the hiss of the shower. He was still here.

Weak with relief, she hugged the pillow Mark had used. It smelled of him—of them together—and she considered slipping into the shower and joining him. But Mother Nature called. She threw on a robe and hurried downstairs to the powder room off the living room. By the time she washed her hands, the shower was silent.

What a shame. Glancing in the mirror, Stacy finger-combed her messy hair and noted the new love bite on her neck, not far from the faded one from the night of the barbecue. She opened her robe to reveal another near her nipple, and one more, just south of her navel. She remembered that one very well, Mark stopping there when she desperately needed his attentions lower down.

Finally, he'd given in to her shameless begging…. The very memory turned her body to liquid heat. She smiled dreamily. Pleased that Mark's passion marked her well-loved body in such a visual way, she closed her robe and tied the sash.

He'd also marked her in ways no one would ever see. With his hands and his body, giving her pleasure and filling her heart with warmth and joy, again and again. Who'd have guessed he possessed the stamina to make love with her multiple times in the space of one night?

Her body was sore from all that sex, but she didn't mind. If Mark wanted her again this morning, she'd gladly accommodate.

"Awk! Stacy, Stacy, Stacy! ST loves you."

"I love you, too, Smooth Talker." Humming, she uncovered the bird. "Did you sleep well?"

"Awk! Feed ST."

"Of course."

After Stacy filled the bird's food dish and changed his water, she left the cage door open so that he could move to his perch in front of the window. Then she padded into the kitchen.

The coffeemaker was bubbling away, filling the kitchen with the heady aroma of French roast, when Mark wandered in, his loafers clomping over the tile floor. The shoes meant he wasn't staying. Stacy bit back her disappointment.

At the very sight of him, his hair wet from the shower and his cheeks and jaw dark with new beard, a deep emotion flooded her.

Risky as it was, she was in love with Mark Engle—feelings she intended to keep to herself.

"Good morning," she said in a perky voice.

"Morning." He bent down to kiss her.

The brief press of his lips to hers set her on fire, but she never had the chance to melt against him. He let her go to rub his chin with his thumb and forefinger. "Don't want to give you a beard burn. I really need a shave."

"I don't have a man's razor," she said, "but you're welcome to borrow mine."

"No, thanks. I'll shave at home."

Stacy nodded. "The coffee is just about ready. What would you like for breakfast? I'm thinking about making pancakes from scratch."

She expected him to grin or lick his lips. Instead, he shook his head. "Can't. I have plans to go hiking with Cody Naylor in about—" he glanced at his watch "—forty-five minutes."

"Oh." Her spirits plummeted. She didn't recall Mark mentioning that, but then he hadn't intended to spend the night. "Do you have time for a quick cup of coffee?" she asked, feigning a nonchalance she didn't feel.

"Wish I did, but I really need to get home."

"We never did eat that chocolate cake," she said, stopping just short of inviting him to come back later. If he wanted to see her tonight, he'd ask. Tomorrow was Memorial Day, so the clinic was closed. He could stay over again. "With your sweet tooth, I know you'll like it."

"Trust me, I got my sweets last night." The corners of Mark's mouth lifted and his eyes glinted warmly. "Good food and you. Last night was the best."

Her heart filled with love and tenderness. "It *was* pretty wonderful. *You* were wonderful." *I love you, Mark Engle.*

Heat and need sharpened the planes of his face, swiftly replaced by what looked like concern. "We're okay, right? About me staying over last night."

Stacy wasn't sure what he meant. Had he guessed how much she cared? Not wanting to scare him away, she forced a casual smile. "Of course we're okay."

His shoulders seemed to relax and his expression cleared. "That's great. I should go."

To Stacy's disappointment, he didn't ask to come back. Six days and counting before he left town and forgot her.

Unless… *Miracles do happen,* she reminded herself as she accompanied him to the door.

"Have a nice Memorial Day," she said, fishing for information about his plans for the holiday.

"You, too," he said. "Thank you for an unforgettable night. I'll see you Tuesday."

He kissed her lightly, opened the door and left.

Hiding behind the drapes, arms wrapped around her waist, she watched him drive away.

"YOU INVITED MARK TO dinner last night," Dr. Tom said later that afternoon. "He mentioned it when he stopped by yesterday."

He would bring up Mark. Hoping the thoroughly loved glow didn't give her away, Stacy feigned a nonchalant expression. "That's right," she said. "Mark cooked dinner for me the same evening Megan had her baby, and I wanted to pay him back."

"I hadn't heard that he made you dinner. Huh." The old doctor studied Stacy shrewdly, making her wonder if the concealer had worn off her neck. "There's something different about you today. You're lit up like a woman in love."

"Am I?" Afraid Dr. Tom would see the truth in her eyes, she glanced down and smoothed the creases in her lightweight slacks. "Mark mentioned that you're moving into the retirement home outside town. Why didn't you tell me?"

"Go ahead and change the subject, but you can't fool these old eyes," the doctor said amiably. "As for my decision to live at Sunset Manor, I only made up my mind a few days ago. If I continue to improve at the same rate I have been, I'll be out of this place in about a week. I had to move fast. Good thing I did—a one-bedroom just came available. They're cleaning and painting now, and by the time I leave here, it should be ready."

"What amazing timing," Stacy replied. "I'm happy to help you pack." If the miracle she hoped for happened and Mark decided to stay, he could also lend a hand.

"I may take you up on that. Back to you and Mark. Are you in love with him, or not?"

"Dr. Tom! That's really none of your business."

Undaunted, the doctor nodded. "You *are*."

Stacy had never been with a man as generous and caring as Mark. She wanted to spend her life with him, and obviously wasn't as good at hiding her feelings as she'd hoped. She sighed. "I haven't known him very long."

"That doesn't matter. One hour after meeting Celia, may she rest in peace, I knew she was the woman for me."

"That fast?"

"For me, it was. She wasn't convinced, though. We dated for six months before she accepted my marriage proposal. We married on the anniversary of our first meeting, and shared forty wonderful years together. So yes, Stacy, with the right person, true love can happen fast."

It definitely had—for Stacy. She wasn't at all sure about Mark.

SEATED WITH HIS BACK AGAINST a twisted tree along the Calypso Trail, Mark swigged a long drink of water and watched a hawk soar across the endless sky. After a rugged four-hour hike, he was thirsty and hungry. "This is beautiful country," he said, before tearing into a ham sandwich.

"One of my favorite places in the world." Sitting cross-legged near a jagged chunk of shale, Cody drank a large swig of water, then wiped his mouth with his sleeve.

Bitterroots were the Montana state flower, and Mark recognized the lavender-hued plants dotting the ground. "Stacy likes wildflowers. She'd like these bitterroots."

"Is that so?" Cody raised his eyebrows and bit into his PB and J.

"What?" Mark asked.

"I'm guessing you two were together last night."

"Who told you that?"

"So you were with her." Cody gave a knowing nod. "When I saw you with her at the Masons' barbecue last weekend, I figured that sooner or later you'd get together."

"What are you talking about?" Mark said. "We hardly said two words to each other that night."

"Yeah, but it was obvious that you were hot for each other."

Mark glared at his hiking buddy. "If you know what's good for you, you'll wipe that smirk off your face."

Cody shrugged. "I think it's interesting, that's all. You're the first guy she's even looked at since she moved here. She's really into you."

"I like her, too," Mark admitted. *Too much.*

"I took her out once."

The thought of Stacy with big, good-looking Cody Naylor did not sit well. Mark narrowed his eyes. "Did you sleep with her?"

Cody rolled his eyes. "It was months before you came to town, and we only went out the one time, so cool down. No, I didn't sleep with her. I did kiss her, but there was no spark between us. We're casual friends and that's it."

Mark relaxed and polished off the rest of his sandwich.

"What's going to happen when you leave town next Saturday?" Cody asked as they packed their trash into their backpacks.

"Hopefully some other doctor takes over the clinic, because I can't stay any longer."

"I mean, what's going to happen with Stacy? She's good people, and I don't want to see her hurt."

Neither did Mark. As they reached a steep decline, he

frowned. "Look, I've been straight with her all along. She knows I'm not interested in a relationship right now."

Cody eyed him. "You sure about that?"

Hell, no, which was why he was out of sorts. Not about to share this with Naylor, Mark started down the slope at a fast clip. He stepped on a loose chunk of sandstone, lost his footing and landed hard on his ass. The rock bounced ahead of him down the trail, until it skittered into the scrub.

Swearing, he pushed himself up and dusted off his backside.

Cody roared with laughter—until he got a look at Mark's expression. Sobering quickly, he offered a hand up. "You okay?"

Ignoring Cody's outstretched arm, Mark scrambled up. "Everything but my pride."

During the rest of the hike, neither of them mentioned Stacy again. But Mark thought about her. She knew there was nothing between them. Hell, they'd discussed the matter several times.

All along, she'd stated plainly enough that she wanted more than just a short-term physical relationship. Then suddenly last night, she'd up and changed her mind?

Stupidly, he hadn't thought to question the about-face, mainly because she was so damn desirable and he'd been too focused on the sex.

Which was why his conscience was giving him grief. He thought back to this morning. Stacy *had* seemed disappointed that he couldn't stay for breakfast, but she'd also assured him that she was okay about spending the night together.

Now he had to wonder.

The rest of the day and all of Memorial Day, he went round and round what had happened, mentally smacking himself for letting his groin call the shots.

In the wee hours of Monday morning, he finally figured

out what to do. Before the clinic opened its doors, he had to make sure he and Stacy were reading from the same page. Once again, they needed to talk.

MARK MADE THE COFFEE AND waited for Stacy to show up Tuesday morning. She arrived at her usual time, clutching a metal cake carrier in her arms.

He couldn't see what was inside, but his sweet tooth jumped to life. "What's this?" he asked, temporarily setting any serious conversation aside.

"The cake I made the other night. I smell coffee." She brushed past him. "I hope it's ready, because I haven't had any this morning and I need a huge cup."

"You and me both." Mark accompanied her to the kitchen. "Chocolate cake, right?"

"Chocolate icebox cake."

"Sounds good." Even if it was early morning.

"Help yourself." She thrust the container at him, then reached for the mugs.

The second Mark unhooked and removed the lid, the smell of chocolate enveloped him. Licking his lips, he grabbed a knife from a drawer. He sliced a large wedge for himself. "Want some?"

"No, thanks," she said with her back to him. "It's all yours."

With terse movements, she filled the mugs. The very air felt thick with tension.

She was definitely upset. Mark's conscience reared its ugly head. He forgot the cake. "About the other night..." he started.

"It happened. I wanted to make love as much as you did, so don't feel that you owe me anything," Stacy said, placing her lunch in the fridge. Still, she sounded miffed.

"I don't go around spending the night with just any woman, Stacy," he said. "I stayed because I like you. A lot."

That was true, but not exactly the "we both know this can't go anywhere" speech he'd intended to give.

At least he had her attention. The light in her eyes made his confession worth something.

"That goes both ways," she said. "I'm glad you stayed."

Everything was fine. Mark let out the breath he'd been holding. He'd worried for nothing. "Do you think I could come over again tonight?" he asked, hoping for another amazing night together.

All that warmth vanished, and her back straightened. "When we haven't spoken since you left Sunday morning, not even a phone call from you? I don't think so."

Now he understood why she was mad. "I was a jerk not to call, and I apologize. After the hike Sunday, Cody and I stopped for dinner and I didn't get back until late. I thought about calling you yesterday, but the truth is, I wasn't sure what to say."

"For starters, how about 'thanks for a wonderful night together'?"

She made it sound so easy. "It was a mind-blowing night I'll never forget," he said, letting his intimate gaze underscore the words. "Thank you for the great meal. And for everything else."

The phone rang before Stacy had a chance to reply. "First day back from a three-day weekend and here we go," she said, already on her way to the waiting room. "By the way, that cake should be refrigerated."

She left Mark in the kitchen with the uneasy feeling that his apology had somehow fallen short.

THE MORNING WAS AS BUSY as Stacy had predicted. Juggling phone calls, appointments and walk-ins left her scant moments to puzzle over this morning.

She'd come in, upset with Mark for not calling her, but

he'd surprised her with exactly what she'd needed to hear. *I don't go around spending the night with just any woman, Stacy. I stayed because I like you. A lot.*

An admission followed by an intimate, caring look that had taken her breath away and crowded out any misgivings. Then without a moment's thought, he'd invited himself over for more sex, ruining what had been an emotional and tender moment.

He'd quickly backtracked with an apology and the unbelievable claim he hadn't called because he hadn't known what to say to her. What did he think she wanted, a marriage proposal? This wasn't the Dark Ages—though she *did* want a future with him. Stacy shook her head. Mark's behavior was confusing, to say the least.

Shortly before lunch, the phone rang yet again, but this call wasn't patient related.

"This is Wayne from the physicians' temp agency, calling with good news," the recruiter said. "Great news actually. I located a qualified candidate for the temporary job at your clinic." He gave Stacy the particulars.

"Dr. Tom will be so pleased," she said. "I'd like to tell him about this before you do. As soon as I reach him, I'll phone you back."

When she hung up, she didn't know whether to sigh with relief or cry. Finding a temp meant that for now, the clinic was safe. Mark was free to leave.

Stacy now knew he cared about her. He also cared about the clinic, but she wouldn't hold her breath that those feelings made one whit of difference to his plans—or so she told herself. Deep down, a tiny part of her still clung to the hope that a miracle could happen, and he'd decide to stay.

The last patient of the morning waved and exited the building, leaving the waiting room empty until either a walk-in showed up or the one o'clock arrived. Wanting to eat before she broke the news to Mark, Stacy grabbed her lunch from the refrigerator and pulled the old quilt from the closet.

She was sitting in the shade of the two poplars, picking at her chef's salad and thinking about Mark, when he wandered outside with his own lunch.

Squinting in the bright sunlight, he approached her. "Mind if I join you?"

"Make yourself comfortable," she said, anxious to gauge his reaction to the news from the recruiter.

He sat down near her. "That cake you brought in—outstanding."

"It was a great-aunt's recipe, and has always been one my favorites."

Stacy pulled a banana from her lunch sack and unpeeled it. Mark watched her every move, his gaze heating until his eyes smoldered. As if he was remembering what she did with him the other night.

Men. Saving the banana for later, she tugged her skirt lower and crossed her legs at the ankle. She frowned at her feet. The polish on one big toe was chipped. That she hadn't noticed until now just showed how distracted she'd been.

"I need to tell you something," she said.

About to bite into his lunch, Mark paused. "What's that?"

"A few minutes ago, Wayne from the temp agency called. He found a doctor willing to take a temporary position here." Stacy carefully measured Mark's reaction.

He barely hesitated. "Fantastic."

His enthusiastic tone was at odds with his shuttered expression—or at least it seemed that way to Stacy. Daring to hope, she toyed with her napkin.

"What did Dr. Tom say?"

"I haven't told him yet." The truth was, she'd first wanted to let Mark know, in case he changed his mind.

"He'll be relieved," Mark said. "I know I am."

With that, Stacy knew he'd never even remotely considered staying in Saddlers Prairie.

Sick to her stomach but determined to hide her true feelings, she smiled. "I'm certainly happy about it," she replied in her perkiest voice. "And just in the nick of time."

Unable to eat another bite, she snapped the lid of her lunch container with a loud click. "I'm so excited that I think I'll call Dr. Tom right now."

She was on hold, waiting for the receptionist to ring the doctor's room, when Mark brought in the folded quilt. They smiled at each other, and she gestured toward the closet. He stowed the quilt there, then pointed upstairs.

The instant he disappeared, Stacy's smile crumpled. She'd been a fool.

Mark had never promised her anything, assuring her from the start that he was eager to begin his life in L.A.

But had she listened? No, she'd invested her hopes and heart in a pipe dream.

Miracles didn't happen. Not in her life.

Chapter Eighteen

Mark couldn't believe how fast the news traveled. By the time the clinic reopened after lunch, patients were already buzzing with the announcement that Tom's temporary replacement had been found. And Stacy had barely notified Tom.

Rumor had it, the matter was settled. Which wasn't true, since Tom hadn't even spoken with the recruiter. The premature reaction settled heavily in Mark's gut.

Stacy and Tom knew nothing about this new doctor, and had no idea whether he or she was right for the job. Some physicians lacked people skills, and a surly attitude wouldn't sit well with the citizens of Saddlers Prairie.

This lack of information was what most bothered Mark—or so he told himself. Never mind that Tom and Stacy hadn't known him, either, when he'd stepped in.

Then again, who they hired wasn't his concern. What mattered was, they'd found a replacement. Mark could leave for L.A. knowing he hadn't let them down.

Then why was he so damn cross?

Stacy buzzed him. "Sarah Jane and Byron are here," she told him in the crisp office-manager voice he'd come to know and dread.

Remembering Sarah Jane's anger toward Byron, Mark said, "Send one of them back."

"They want to see you together," she replied.

They entered Mark's office looking much better than the last time they'd visited. "How are you feeling?" he asked.

Sarah Jane spoke first. "My sore throat is gone, but I get tired a lot."

Mark checked her throat and her lymph glands. "You're looking good, Sarah Jane. I'm clearing you to go back to school tomorrow. You're going to be tired for a while, so be sure to get extra rest."

"Can I go back to work at my after-school job?"

"As long as it doesn't wear you out too much. Give it a try and see how you feel."

He turned to Byron. "What about you, Byron?"

"I'm about the same as Sarah Jane."

Mark also cleared the boy for school and work. "Last time I saw you two, you weren't getting along."

The couple exchanged loving glances, and Byron put his arm around Sarah Jane. "We worked everything out. We're okay now, Dr. Mark. I love Sarah Jane so much, and I'll do anything to keep her love. I can wait to have sex until she's ready."

Sarah Jane gave her boyfriend a tender, loving look. "I know how much Byron loves me now. He'd never cheat on me."

The lovey-dovey display put Mark in a worse mood than before, and he nodded at the door. "If your jobs tire you out too much, let me know and I'll write a note to your employers."

They nodded, but neither moved.

"We heard about the new doctor," Byron said.

Mark stifled the urge to roll his eyes.

"We like you, Dr. Mark," the boy continued. "You treat us different than other adults, like we're just as important."

Sarah Jane bit her lip. "We don't want you to leave."

Gratified at their kind words, Mark managed a smile and

accompanied them to the waiting room. No other patients were there, signaling a gap in the schedule.

"You're great kids, and I've enjoyed getting to know you," he said.

Byron held out his hand to shake. "We'll never forget you, or your great advice."

Mark glanced at Stacy, who was watching the exchange, but her face gave away none of her thoughts.

"We wish Dr. Mark would stay," Sarah Jane told her.

"Yes, but he can't," Stacy replied without a glance in Mark's direction. "He's taken a job in Los Angeles." She smiled broadly at the couple—too broadly, Mark thought. "I'm glad you two worked out your differences."

The way she uttered the words made Mark think they were directed at him, even though her total focus was on Byron and Sarah Jane.

Holding hands, the couple left.

Instead of returning to his office to update the patient files, Mark lingered. "There go two of my favorite patients," he said. "I think I'll warm up this morning's coffee. Can I bring you a cup?"

"No, thanks." Stacy glanced at something on her desk and began inputting data into the computer.

"What are you doing?" he asked.

"Compiling the end-of-the-month expense report for Will Borden."

"I didn't know you handled that," Mark said. "You really are indispensable around here."

"I like to think so. We need a software program that compiles everything, but I haven't gotten around to ordering one."

When he lingered, she threw him a questioning look. "Did you need something?"

"I hope the physician who takes my place is good with people," he said.

"I assume he will be."

"So he's male."

"That's right." Her gaze darted between a page of her own handwritten notes and the keyboard. "His name is Dr. Jason Flynn, and he's the same age as you."

Mark didn't like that, but couldn't have said why. "Married?" he asked, careful to keep his tone nonchalant.

"I don't know, but I'm sure Dr. Tom will find out. They've scheduled a phone interview for tomorrow morning." She frowned. "I thought you wanted coffee."

"I do," Mark said, but his feet stayed planted in front of Stacy's desk. "Speaking of Tom, has he called for me this afternoon?"

She shook her head.

The old doctor hadn't even bothered to notify Mark about Jason Flynn. Stung, he fired off another question. "What else do you know about this guy?"

Her eyes widened, making her look both innocent and slightly irritated. "Why are you so interested in Dr. Jason?"

Hell if Mark knew. He shifted his weight. "Just curious."

"This is what the recruiter told me." Stacy opened the middle drawer and pulled out a piece of paper that was filled with penned notes. "Dr. Jason Flynn earned his M.D. in family practice from Jefferson Medical College in Philadelphia. He recently finished a fellowship in pediatrics at Case Western. His family once vacationed in Montana and he's eager to come back." She returned the paper to the drawer. "I don't know about you, but I'm sold."

"You're talking like Tom already hired this guy," Mark grumbled.

"As you and I both know, he has no choice. We're just lucky that working at our clinic seems like the right fit for Dr. Jason and for our patients."

Saddlers Prairie would have a new doctor who sounded

pretty damn perfect. Mark waited for a flood of relief. Instead his gut tied up in knots.

The reason sat before him, typing away.

Stacy. Beautiful, desirable, passionate.

And she was his—or she had been, for one phenomenal night.

Oblivious of his thoughts, she went on. "Who knows, maybe he'll like Saddlers Prairie. Maybe *his* life plan is to stay here permanently."

She flashed a phony smile that all but screamed "unlike yours."

Over the years, other people had knocked the fact that he'd made and followed a plan for his life, but he'd never let it bother him.

This time was different. "Don't diss my plan," he said. "Sticking with it has literally saved my life."

But that'd been before Stacy. Mark pushed the thought away. Letting go of the plan he'd relied on all these years scared him as much as giving up oxygen.

"For the record," he added, "I happen to *like* Saddlers Prairie."

Stacy didn't appear to have heard. She returned to her work, the keyboard click-clacking as her fingers flew across it.

Seconds later, she frowned at the screen. "Darn it, I lost my place. If you'll excuse me, I'd like to finish this now, so that I can leave on time tonight." *Tap-tap, tappity-tap.*

Mark put his hands up. "Okay, all right. I'll be in the kitchen. Let me know when my next patient arrives."

"Will do." Humming, Stacy typed away.

She seemed pleased about Jason Flynn. She liked Mark, yet she didn't seem at all sorry to see him go. Talk about your major downer.

Mentally scratching his head, he glumly pulled a mug

from the cabinet. While waiting for the microwave to beep, he admitted the truth to himself. As much as he wanted the job in L.A., he was torn up about leaving Stacy. He wasn't thrilled about leaving Sarah Jane and Byron, the Dawsons, Anita and many other patients he'd gotten to know, either.

In the short time he'd been here he'd come to care deeply for Stacy, and was pretty sure he wanted her in his life—someday. Right now he needed to focus on the next step in his plan—becoming a future partner in Archer Clinic.

But there was no reason why he couldn't keep in touch, and even invite her to visit. If that worked out, then at some point he'd ask her to move to L.A. and see what happened. That way, he wouldn't have to give up Stacy or his plan. He decided to keep that option to himself for now.

Pleased with himself for hatching such a great idea, he grinned.

BEFORE DAWN WEDNESDAY, the skies opened and spilled much-needed rain on the parched Montana earth. Knowing how badly the garden needed water after several weeks of hot sun, Stacy welcomed the downpour. The weatherman predicted a full day of storms, and patients talked in worried voices of possible flooding.

By the time the last of the morning appointments finally cleared out of the office, her stomach was empty and growling. She really needed a break from the clinic, but with only twenty minutes before the next appointment, leaving wasn't possible. Since she'd forgotten an umbrella, she couldn't even run to her car without getting drenched.

She was seated at the café table with her lunch and a book, when Mark ambled into the kitchen.

"Busy morning," he said. "How was Tom's interview with the new guy?"

Though he leaned against the wall in a casual pose, tension radiated from him. Apparently, her answer mattered a great deal to him.

Stacy frowned. He had no stake in Saddlers Prairie Clinic, so why should he care? "Very good, from what Dr. Tom said. He liked Dr. Jason, especially when he agreed to start a week from Monday instead of waiting the usual two weeks."

"Great, but this Friday is my last day. That leaves the clinic without a doctor for a full week. You'll have to close the doors, unless… Tom isn't making noises about me staying on an extra week, is he?"

The deliberate, blank expression on Mark's face was all the more confusing. Did he *want* Dr. Tom to beg him to stay? Stacy couldn't imagine why, since Mark and his new boss had agreed on a start date next week.

"Don't worry, Mark, you're off the hook. We're going to close for a week. The patients will be inconvenienced, but Dr. Tom okayed it."

Stacy kept her tone light, but inside she was falling apart. Mark was leaving, and he hadn't said one word about keeping in touch. She doubted she'd ever see him again.

"Actually, I'm relieved about the temporary closure," she bubbled on. "I'll be able to help Dr. Tom move and get him settled into his apartment at Sunset Manor. I'll also have time to get the apartment upstairs ready for Dr. Jason." Something made her add, "Oh, and by the way, he's single."

Mark's forbidding frown made her wonder if he were jealous. *That* lifted her flagging spirits. "I'll probably go to Spenser's this weekend and look for new bedding and linens for him," she said.

"Bedding," Mark repeated in a growl.

Definitely jealous. For the first time in days, Stacy smiled.

Chapter Nineteen

A hard run in the driving rain early Wednesday evening did nothing to lighten Mark's dour mood. By the time he sprinted to the front door of the clinic, he was so wet his shoes squeaked. Naturally, as soon as he shut the door behind him, the sky cleared.

No one seemed to care that he was leaving Saddlers Prairie for good. Sure, he'd been here only a few weeks, but people had seemed to like him and he'd assumed they appreciated his friendliness and healing skills. Now the turncoats were talking up his replacement.

Tom hadn't even had the decency to pick up the phone and thank him for his time. And Stacy... Mark had no idea as to her thoughts.

After a shower and an insipid microwaved dinner, he tromped to his car, too antsy to sit home and brood.

Moments later, he was headed for Anita's salon on the edge of town for a much-needed haircut. He wasn't sure she worked after 6:00 p.m., or why he couldn't wait a few more days and get his hair cut in L.A.

The little lot in front of the tiny wood building that housed Anita's Hair Salon was empty, save for an old sedan. As Mark slid his compact into a parking slot, Anita was just locking the door.

Muttering, he started to back out, but she saw him and

waved. He lowered his window. "You said to stop by when I wanted a cut, but I can see you're through for the night."

"No problem, Dr. Mark. I'm delighted you're here. Just let me call the sitter and let her know I'll be late."

"You sure?"

"Miss a chance to cut Dr. Mark Engle's hair? Never! Please, come in."

Her salon was like any other, with hair products on the shelves, photos of various styles for both men and women hanging on the walls, a hair dryer and a big black sink. While Anita made her call, Mark took one of the four chairs for waiting customers and idly glanced through the magazines on the coffee table.

Minutes later, Anita gestured him to the sink. "Let's wash your hair."

"I just did," he said.

"Okay, but I still need to wet it." She draped a plastic cape around his torso. "Lie back, Dr. Mark. I heard about the doctor Stacy and Dr. Tom hired to replace you," she went on as she sprayed warm water over his head.

"Yep, it looks as if they found someone." Mark sat up, and she toweled and combed his hair.

"They say he's a hotshot bachelor who wants the experience of living in a small town. How do you want your hair styled?"

"Just cut it."

"All right." She began to snip the ends. "I wonder if the new doctor will be interested in a relationship with an attractive local woman."

Mark met her reflection in the mirror with narrowed eyes. "What the hell does *that* mean?"

The busy scissors stilled. "You don't think I'm attractive?" Anita asked, pouting.

She was talking about herself, not Stacy. Mark relaxed. "You're very pretty."

"Thanks." As Anita traded the scissors for a razor to shave his neck, she eyed him in the mirror. "Ah, *now* I understand. You're worried that Stacy and your replacement will get together."

Bingo.

"If you like her, Doc—and that's pretty obvious—do something about it." She whipped off the plastic cover. "All done. What do you think?"

"It looks fine, thanks." In no mood for advice, Mark handed Anita several bills, but she shook her head.

"This cut is on me, remember?"

"Yeah, but because of me, you have to pay your babysitter extra. This should cover the cost."

"About double. Let me get you some change."

"That's your tip. Keep it."

"Wow. Thanks. Come back anytime, Dr. Mark. I sure hate to see you go."

At the door, Anita opened her arms. He had no choice but to let her hug him. "I don't think I'll see you before you leave. Travel safely, and remember little Saddlers Prairie. I'm not the only one who's going to miss you."

The words lifted Mark's spirits. He intended to head back to the apartment and start packing, but his car had other ideas. Before he knew it, he was pulling into Stacy's driveway.

STANDING ON HER BACK STOOP, Stacy toed out of her muddy sneakers. After a satisfying hour spent yanking weeds from the wet garden and cursing herself for falling in love with Mark, she felt pretty good.

Suddenly Smooth Talker squawked. "Awk! Look sharp, look sharp!"

Someone was at the front door, but who? Sweaty and dirty,

she quickly rinsed her hands in the sink. Wiping her palms on the thighs of her gardening sweats, she padded in her socks through the dining room. When she reached the front door and opened it, Mark stood on the step.

"Hi," he said.

Stacy frowned. "What are you doing here?"

He seemed taken aback by the question. "Anita just gave me a haircut, and I wanted to see you. You look great."

His gaze traveled over her tank top and loose sweatpants, bringing with it the familiar heat. She started to melt, then caught herself. If she wanted to get over Mark, she couldn't do that anymore.

"No, I don't," she said. Avoiding his gaze, she glanced down at her unflattering, dirt-streaked outfit. "I'm sweaty and half-covered in mud."

"I like you this way."

Had he been drinking? Stacy sniffed the air, but didn't smell alcohol.

"We need to talk," he said. "Gonna let me in?"

The very thought of having Mark in the house when her feelings were so bruised made Stacy nervous. Yet she was also curious. What did he want to talk about? The instant she stepped aside, he crossed the threshold into the house.

For one long moment, he said nothing, just stood silently in her tiny entry, big and imposing with his dark, intent gaze. Impossible to read and difficult to resist.

Stacy backed away. "I need to change out of these clothes." And compose herself so that she didn't do something foolish like blurt out her feelings.

She didn't get far before Mark caught hold of her wrist. "Don't go. You're fine."

"Awk! Watch it, you two-fisted shit bastard," Smooth Talker scolded.

Silently thanking the parrot, Stacy pulled out of Mark's grasp. "I'm too dirty to sit down."

"So we'll both stand. This won't take long."

His warm expression rekindled the hope she'd thought had died. Had he changed his mind and decided to stay in Saddlers Prairie? Hardly daring to breathe, she waited.

This time when he reached for her hands, she willingly took hold. "What's this about, Mark?"

"I want you to come to L.A.—after I get the chance to prove myself."

He wanted her with him? Surprise and joy rendered her speechless. But live in L.A.? Before Stacy could form a single thought, he went on.

"Until then, I'll be working extra-long hours. If all goes according to plan, in a year or two, when the other partners know me well enough, I should be able to cut back to more normal hours. Then I want you to fly to L.A. and join me."

In other words, Mark expected her to wait until *he* was ready. She'd done that once already—wasted far too much time setting her dreams aside to accommodate someone else's timeline.

Mark hadn't even said he loved her. True, he'd admitted he liked her, but she couldn't build a life with him based on that.

She moved past him into the living room, where they could talk without standing nose to nose. "One to two years is a long time to wait. So much can happen."

He could change his mind or invent some new timeline that dragged out even further. Worse, he might meet someone else. The idea sickened Stacy, but if Mark didn't love her, it could easily happen.

"You know how I feel about L.A.," she said. "It's a great place to visit, but living there again doesn't appeal to me."

"It would if we were together."

Not this way. Stacy shook her head. "Saddlers Prairie is my home. I love this town and my house, and I love my job."

"Will you at least think about it?" Mark asked, earnestly searching her face.

"Will you consider living in Saddlers Prairie, and taking over our clinic?" she countered. His answer would tell her everything she needed to know. "It's not too late to change your mind."

If he truly cared for her, he'd at least consider the option.

But Mark didn't even pause before he shook his head. "I can't do that, Stacy. I accepted a job in L.A., a great position with potential in spades." He crossed his arms. "That's where I want to be."

Stacy's heart broke, but at least she knew where she stood—in second place behind someone else's career. She'd been there before. But this time she wouldn't make the same mistakes.

"Do you know what I think?" she said. "That sticking to your life plan is an excuse to avoid real intimacy. Your previous two girlfriends knew it, and so do I."

When Mark said nothing, she released a heavy breath. "I guess we're at an impasse. Good night, Mark."

Chapter Twenty

Mark had laid all his cards on the table for Stacy, and she'd rejected him. That's what happened when he deviated from his plan. He swore at his stupidity.

Worse still, Stacy had accused him of using his life plan to avoid intimacy. Feeling let down and confused, he drove straight to the hospital to see Tom.

At nearly nine-thirty, the cardio-rehab wing was relatively quiet. He rapped on Tom's closed door.

"Come in."

The old doctor was seated in a chair, reading a book. He pushed his glasses up so that they rested on his thinning hair, and arched his eyebrows. "Kinda late for a visit, isn't it? What if I'd been asleep?"

"You're a night owl, Tom. I knew you'd be awake."

"Only because I retired. If I was still putting in those long days at the clinic, I'd be getting ready to turn in about now." Tom set the book on a small table, then gestured at the other chair in the tiny room. "Sit down, son, and tell me what I can do for you."

"I don't need anything," Mark said. Instead of sitting down, he picked up Tom's book, a hardcover biography, and skimmed the back cover. "This looks interesting."

"I'm enjoying it. So this is a social call, is it?"

His wise eyes seemed to bore into Mark. Mark eyeballed him back. "Why didn't you tell me you hired a doctor?"

"Figured Stacy would. Great news, isn't it?"

"Terrific, but I would've appreciated a courtesy call from *you.*"

"No need to raise your voice, son." Tom frowned. "I thought you'd be happy about it, seeing as you wanted to leave since the day you arrived. Now you can."

"That's right—I can and I will." Mark gripped the book so hard his fingers ached, earning more scrutiny from Tom. He returned it to the table and began to pace, but the room was so small that he gave up and dropped into the chair.

Several tense seconds ticked by before Tom spoke. "Go on, son, get it off your chest."

With that invitation, Mark did. "You haven't pressured me to take over for you."

"Sure I have, and so did the mayor. But you have your future all mapped out, and it doesn't include Saddlers Prairie." Tom's eyes narrowed a fraction. "Are you telling me you changed your mind and want to stay?"

Mark refused to even consider the possibility. "No," he said.

"Maybe I'm missing something, because I don't understand."

"You're not the only one," Mark muttered.

Tom squinted, then nodded sagely. "This is about Stacy, isn't it? What are you doing wasting your time with me? If you want her, go after her."

"I tried, but she refuses to move to L.A."

"You asked her to move down there?"

"Less than an hour ago. She turned me down flat, chose Saddlers Prairie over me." Mark couldn't get over that.

"You sure there aren't other reasons why she turned you down?"

"She accused me of using my life plan to avoid intimacy," he said.

What if she were right?

The thought scared Mark witless. For his own peace of mind, for the sake of his very survival, he needed to stay the course.

"I see. Did she ask you to live in Saddlers Prairie?"

Mark nodded. "But she knows I can't do that."

"Can't or won't?"

"They're holding the job for me in L.A."

"True, but a place like Archer could easily find someone else."

"But they chose me," Mark said. "I have a chance of becoming a partner there. You don't get an opportunity like that every day."

Tom tapped his finger thoughtfully against his lips. "Let me ask you a question, son. Which is more important to you, love or this life plan you set up years ago?"

"If Stacy moves to L.A., I can have both."

"But if you had to choose one?"

Unable to do that, Mark shook his head.

The old doctor snorted. "No wonder she turned you down. You have some serious thinking to do."

IT SEEMED TO STACY THAT all day Thursday she and Mark danced around each other. She worked hard at being friendly and civil, he treated her the same way, and all in all, they got along well enough.

On Friday, patients wished him good luck in his new position, while Stacy smiled gamely and fought back the tears. By the time the last patient exited the clinic, she was emotionally drained from pretending to be happy and was in need of a good cry.

Anxious to leave, she closed the drapes and placed the sign

that read Closed Until June 11 in the window. Never mind straightening up. She'd come and do that next week, while the clinic was closed.

By then, Mark would be long gone. Already she missed him, but then she'd missed him for days now, since he'd stopped by her house and she'd known with certainty that he put her second.

Would she *never* learn?

She was pulling herself together to say goodbye and wish him a good life when he entered the waiting room.

Her heart lurched painfully and her eyes threatened to fill. *I will* not *cry.* "I'm just getting ready to leave," she said, attempting a smile and failing.

"It's my last night in town. Have dinner with me." His lips quirked. "We'll go to Barb's."

If that was supposed to be a joke, it wasn't funny. Dinner with Mark anywhere guaranteed that Stacy would fall apart, and she wasn't about to do that in front of him. After all, she had *some* pride. "I really can't," she said.

Regret shadowed his face. "I understand. I'll call you from L.A."

Prolong the heartbreak? Stacy bit her lip. "You probably shouldn't. On your way out tomorrow morning, lock the door and drop the key in the mailbox."

"I don't want to leave things this way, but if that is how you want it…" He touched her face with melting tenderness.

Hastily Stacy blinked back the tears. "Goodbye, Mark. I hope you'll be very happy in your new life."

His hand dropped to his side. "Goodbye, Stacy. I'll never forget you or these past few weeks."

Neither would she, and she had the broken heart to prove it. "Travel safely." She hurried out the door.

She'd barely reached the highway before the tears started. Afraid to drive, she pulled over and cried until her eyes ached.

When at last she blew her nose and headed back onto the road, she promised herself that, in time, she'd get over Mark Engle.

MARK WAITED TEN DAYS after moving before picking up the phone to call Stacy. She'd asked him not to contact her, but he needed to hear her voice. He also wanted to know about Dr. Tom, whether Sara Jane and Byron had come back in, how Graham Dawson and the rest of the family were, and about a dozen other people in Saddlers Prairie.

Seated on the comfortable sofa in his spacious apartment that felt too big and too quiet, he dialed her number after dark, when he knew she'd finished gardening for the night.

The phone rang six times. Swallowing disappointment, he was about to hang up when she finally answered.

"Hello," she said, sounding breathless.

"It's me, Mark. You asked me not to call, and if you want me to hang up, I will."

"Please don't. It's good to hear from you."

At the soft delight in her voice, the tension that coiled tightly in his gut eased. Mark smiled and settled into the cushions. "How are you?"

"At the moment, filthy. I've been outside and was just washing the dirt off my hands."

Mark pictured her in her gardening clothes with muddy smudges on her face and his smile widened. "Still pulling those weeds?"

"Like crazy. You wouldn't believe how fast they grow. I swear, sometimes I think the weed fairy sows new shoots while I'm at work. How's life in L.A. and at Archer Clinic?"

"I haven't had much chance to explore the city yet, but I like what I've seen," Mark said, though at night the smog and light pollution masked all but the brightest stars. Well, Stacy had warned him. "I'm putting in even longer hours at the clinic than I imagined, but I'm getting used to it."

"So you like working there."

Mark thought about Archer, where the support staff were helpful and friendly enough, but his peers openly competed, striving to outdo one another. Many of the patients seemed whiny and demanding—he was coming to learn that wasn't unusual for the super rich. He couldn't say he was happy, but he was determined.

"It's growing on me," he said.

"That's good. I'm glad for you, Mark."

She sounded sincere, and he imagined her eyes shining with that special Stacy warmth. God above, he wished she were sitting beside him so that he could hold her.

"Jason Flynn started today. How'd that go?" What he really wanted to know was whether Stacy was attracted to his replacement.

"He doesn't handle walk-ins well, and we had a bunch throughout the day, so things were a little rough. But he'll adapt." She made a noise that sounded like a forced laugh. "He'll have to."

"Other than that, do you like the guy?"

"He's okay, but he's not you."

Feeling better by the minute, Mark asked about various patients. Stacy regaled him with stories, making him laugh. He felt better than he had since leaving Saddlers Prairie.

"How's Tom doing?" he asked.

"This past weekend, a couple of us moved him into Sunset Manor. That was a big job. His new apartment is smaller than the one above the clinic, but it's clean and nice, and he seems to like it. We ran into several friends and former patients who now live there, and he was pleased about that. Let's just hope he stays that way."

Mark chuckled. "If Tom's unhappy, you're sure to hear all about it."

"Loud and clear. He'd better not change his mind and move

again, because I'm already planning a surprise seventy-fifth birthday party there. This year, his birthday falls on Labor Day, and with the Manor's okay, I'm going to invite everyone in town for a potluck dinner there. I figure Dr. Tom should be allowed to eat whatever he wants on his special day, and I'll ask guests to bring their favorite home-cooked dish instead of a present."

"He'll get a kick out of that," Mark said. "Opal Farraday will probably make one of her pies." He licked his lips.

"I'm hoping Silas will bring a platter of spicy barbecued ribs."

"You're making my mouth water." Mark almost wished he could be there. He missed Tom, Saddlers Prairie and all the people he'd met.

Most of all, he missed Stacy. "I think about you a lot," he said.

"Me, too."

The moments of silence that ticked by felt thick with emotion.

"Awk! Feed ST."

"Be patient," Stacy scolded the bird. "You'd think he hadn't eaten all day. He wants attention and his treat."

Mark even missed the cranky parrot. "Tell him hello from me." He cleared his throat. "I'll phone you again in a few days."

"I'd like that."

He began to call after work several nights a week, often chatting while he ate takeout—he rarely had time to cook. Between calls, he and Stacy emailed and texted. She kept him apprised of the people he knew and some he'd never met. The patients hadn't taken to Jason Flynn as quickly as they had to Mark, but were grudgingly adjusting.

After working in a clinic that seemed crazier and more hectic by the day, the conversations with Stacy kept him sane.

He enjoyed her every word, but listening to her stories wasn't enough. Damned if he wasn't homesick for Saddlers Prairie. He'd sure never missed Steer Bluff.

As often as he and Stacy talked, neither of them brought up the future. Mark thought about it a lot, though. As their conversations brought them closer, he understood that she was right. He'd used his life plan and work as an excuse to avoid real intimacy.

Accepting the truth opened the door to other insights. Life was unpredictable and messy, and had been especially so during his childhood. Making a plan was a control mechanism, a way to avoid the awful chaos.

But this time, his need for control had steered him in the wrong direction—away from Stacy.

In the past the insight would've scared him. It no longer did. He was closer to her than he'd ever been to anyone, and he wanted to grow even closer. He wanted her in his life now and forever, living in the same house, cooking meals together, talking about their days and making sweet love at night.

He was in love with her.

The realization both startled and excited him. But Stacy didn't want to live in L.A., and Mark wasn't sure how to make it work.

Meanwhile, he continued at Archer Clinic, working hard to adjust and settle in, but never quite feeling as if he fit. Ten weeks into the job, he admitted to himself that he was miserable. He accepted that leaving Saddlers Prairie to join the clinic had been a mistake. But how to fix the problem?

Maybe it was time to let go of his life plan and trust himself to make the right decisions. The once-terrifying idea felt oddly freeing. Especially when he understood that Stacy, not any plan, was all he needed for a good and happy life.

Mark threw back his head and laughed, the joyous sound echoing in his otherwise silent apartment. Feeling like a bird about to fly from a cliff, he spread his metaphorical wings and jumped.

According to Stacy, Jason Flynn was talking about staying in Saddlers Prairie permanently, making Mark's chances of returning to the local clinic all but impossible.

There must be a way, and Mark knew who might help. He picked up the phone and called Tom.

Labor Day

STACY LED DR. TOM INTO the dining room at Sunset Manor for what he thought was a birthday dinner for the two of them.

Seventy-nine guests awaited him, Jason Flynn notably absent. He'd RSVP'd weeks ago, and Stacy hoped he'd arrive soon.

"Surprise! Happy birthday!" the well-wishers called out.

Stacy laughed at the astonished expression on the old doctor's face. Mark would love this. She'd invited him to the party, but he'd already committed to a medical conference in the Midwest.

She swallowed a lonely sigh. After months of talking on the phone and getting to know him even better than before, she'd fallen more deeply in love with him. They'd actually begun discussing her flying down to visit in the near future.

"Speech! Speech!" the mayor called out, and other guests took up the chant.

Someone handed Dr. Tom a portable microphone, and the room quieted.

"You tricked me, but good." His eyes sparkled and his mouth quirked. "I thank you for this wonderful surprise."

Stacy took the microphone. "There's more, Dr. Tom. Dinner tonight is potluck, courtesy of everyone here. You get to eat whatever you want—doctor's orders."

The guest of honor rubbed his belly, which thanks to daily

walks and careful eating had shrunk by several inches. The room erupted in laughter.

Dr. Tom took back the mic and elbowed Stacy aside. "Now *I* have a surprise for *you,* something not even Stacy knows about. This afternoon, Dr. Jason accepted a job in Philadelphia."

Stacy's jaw dropped. "I thought he was staying in Saddlers Prairie."

"Changed his mind," Dr. Tom said cheerfully.

Aside from Stacy, no one seemed upset. Jason Flynn may have talked about continuing at the clinic, but he'd never really connected with the patients.

"Does this mean you're coming back to work?" Drew Dawson called out.

Alarmed, Stacy frowned. "Don't give him any ideas, Drew."

People started talking all at once. Dr. Tom held up his hands, silencing them. "There's no call to work yourselves into fits," he soothed. "No, I will not be returning to the clinic."

"But without a doctor, there won't *be* a clinic," Val Mason pointed out.

Stacy would lose her job. Then what? She thought of Mark and their deepening relationship. She didn't want to leave Saddlers Prairie, but if he told her he loved her and invited her to move to L.A. again, she just might. Her change of heart surprised her.

"We have a doctor, and a darned fine one—that's the second part of my surprise." Dr. Tom gave a crafty grin, then glanced toward the back of the room. "You can come in now."

The door opened. Mark strode in, tall, handsome and smiling.

Stacy's heart nearly burst from her chest. Around her, people were cheering.

"Join Stacy and me up here, Mark."

With eyes only for Stacy, Mark took his place beside her.

Beaming, Dr. Tom continued. "It is my great pleasure to announce that Dr. Mark Engle has accepted the position of physician at Saddlers Prairie Clinic."

Applause broke out.

"I have an announcement of my own," Mark said over the noise. He waited until the room went silent to continue. "I want you all to hear this from my lips." He turned to Stacy. "I'm crazy about you, Stacy Andrews."

Love flooded her, filling all the empty places and making her giddy. "But what about Archer Clinic, all the money you're making and your chance at a partnership? What about your life plan?"

"I don't need the plan anymore. There are some things money simply can't buy. Friends, love, a place to call home. You. I'm taking you home to meet my mom."

The entire room exploded in applause and loud whoops.

Standing near the front of the room, Anita Eden sniffled. "If that isn't the sweetest thing I ever heard."

From the side of the room, Jenny blew her nose.

Sarah Jane and Byron, who didn't know Dr. Tom but had wanted to come tonight anyway, grinned.

Tears escaped from Stacy's eyes, and Mark looked stricken. "You don't want to be with me," he said.

Stacy laughed. "Are you kidding? You're the man of my dreams. I love you, Mark."

The joy on his face lit up the room. "I feel like the richest man on earth."

Then, in front of everyone, he pulled Stacy close and kissed her.

* * * * *

Watch for the next book in
Ann Roth's SADDLERS PRAIRIE *miniseries,*
HER RANCHER HERO, coming soon,
only from Harlequin American Romance!

HEART & HOME

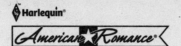

COMING NEXT MONTH
AVAILABLE JULY 10, 2012

#1409 AIDAN: LOYAL COWBOY
Harts of the Rodeo
Cathy McDavid
Can Aidan Hart put aside his responsibilities running the family ranch to deal with his surprise impending fatherhood? Find out in the first book of the Harts of the Rodeo miniseries!

#1410 A BABY ON THE RANCH
Forever, Texas
Marie Ferrarella
Abandoned by her husband, Kasey Stonestreet and her new baby move onto Eli Rodriguez's ranch, where the lifelong friends soon become lovers. *But what will happen when Kasey's husband returns?*

#1411 THE RENEGADE COWBOY RETURNS
Callahan Cowboys
Tina Leonard
Gage Phillips has spent his life as a renegade...until he finds out he has a daughter. Add a feisty Irish redhead who's a natural at motherhood and you have a recipe to tie down the formerly footloose cowboy!

#1412 THE TEXAS RANCHER'S VOW
Legends of Laramie County
Cathy Gillen Thacker
Matt Briscoe suspects the attractive artist hired by his father is hiding something from him. Jen Carson has sworn to keep the elder Briscoe's secret—but how can she, when she's falling in love with Matt?

Lively stories about homes, families and communities like the ones you know. This is romance the all-American way!

REQUEST YOUR FREE BOOKS!

2 FREE NOVELS PLUS 2 FREE GIFTS!

LOVE, HOME & HAPPINESS

YES! Please send me 2 FREE Harlequin® American Romance® novels and my 2 FREE gifts (gifts are worth about $10). After receiving them, if I don't wish to receive any more books, I can return the shipping statement marked "cancel." If I don't cancel, I will receive 4 brand-new novels every month and be billed just $4.49 per book in the U.S. or $5.24 per book in Canada. That's a saving of at least 14% off the cover price! It's quite a bargain! Shipping and handling is just 50¢ per book in the U.S. and 75¢ per book in Canada.* I understand that accepting the 2 free books and gifts places me under no obligation to buy anything. I can always return a shipment and cancel at any time. Even if I never buy another book, the two free books and gifts are mine to keep forever.

154/354 HDN FEP2

Name	(PLEASE PRINT)	
Address		Apt. #
City	State/Prov.	Zip/Postal Code

Signature (if under 18, a parent or guardian must sign)

Mail to the **Reader Service:**
IN U.S.A.: P.O. Box 1867, Buffalo, NY 14240-1867
IN CANADA: P.O. Box 609, Fort Erie, Ontario L2A 5X3

Not valid for current subscribers to Harlequin American Romance books.

Want to try two free books from another line?
Call 1-800-873-8635 or visit www.ReaderService.com.

* Terms and prices subject to change without notice. Prices do not include applicable taxes. Sales tax applicable in N.Y. Canadian residents will be charged applicable taxes. Offer not valid in Quebec. This offer is limited to one order per household. All orders subject to credit approval. Credit or debit balances in a customer's account(s) may be offset by any other outstanding balance owed by or to the customer. Please allow 4 to 6 weeks for delivery. Offer available while quantities last.

Your Privacy—The Reader Service is committed to protecting your privacy. Our Privacy Policy is available online at www.ReaderService.com or upon request from the Reader Service.

We make a portion of our mailing list available to reputable third parties that offer products we believe may interest you. If you prefer that we not exchange your name with third parties, or if you wish to clarify or modify your communication preferences, please visit us at www.ReaderService.com/consumerschoice or write to us at Reader Service Preference Service, P.O. Box 9062, Buffalo, NY 14269. Include your complete name and address.

*Harlequin® American Romance® presents
a new installment in favorite author Tina Leonard's
miniseries* CALLAHAN COWBOYS.

*Enjoy a sneak peek at
THE RENEGADE COWBOY RETURNS.*

The secret to Gage Phillips's happy existence was ridiculously simple: stay far away from women, specifically those who had marriage on the mind.

He put his duffel on the porch of the New Mexico farmhouse and looked around. The rebuilding project he'd taken on for Jonas Callahan was perfectly suited to a man who loved solitude. Gage knew his formula for a drama-free, productive lifestyle was oversimplified to some, especially ladies who wanted to show him how much better his life could be with a good woman. But the fact that he was thirty-five and a die-hard, footloose cowboy only proved his formula was the best choice a man could ever make on this earth, besides choosing the right career and spending hard-earned cash on a dependable truck.

He hadn't always been die-hard and footloose. Fourteen years ago he'd been at the altar, and he'd learned a valuable lesson: marriage was not for him.

His friends were fond of saying he was just too much of a renegade to be tied down. Gage figured they might have a point. Fatherhood had been a late-breaking news bulletin for him about a year ago—what man was so busy traveling the country that he didn't know he had a daughter?

His ex, Leslie, convinced by her parents not to tell him about his child so they wouldn't have to share custody, had made a midlife conscience-cleansing decision to invite him to Laredo to tell him. He was pretty certain she had told him only because she was at her wit's end—and because Cat was apparently fond of making her mother's new boyfriend miserable.

The situation was messy.

"Excuse me," a woman said, and Gage jumped about a foot. "If you're selling something, I'm not buying, cowboy. And there's a No Trespassing sign posted on the drive, which I'm sure you noticed. And ignored."

He'd whipped around at her first words and found himself staring at a female of slender build, with untamable red hair, eyeing him like a protective mother hen prepared to flap him off the porch. Maybe she was the housekeeper, getting the place cleaned up for his arrival. Anyway, she seemed clear that he wasn't getting past the front door. He tried on a convincing smile to let her know he was harmless. "I'm not selling anything, ma'am. I'm moving in."

Who is this woman? Will she let Gage past the front door?

Find out in THE RENEGADE COWBOY RETURNS.
Available this July wherever books are sold.

This summer, celebrate everything Western
with Harlequin® Books!

www.Harlequin.com/Western